Gender Bender
and other underdog stories

By

Kevee Lynch

To Richard
a true legend
and dear friend

Kevee Lynch

In life there will always be an underdog, someone who doesn't quite fit the Status Quo.

Be that person, ignore the haters and follow your own path.

If you have been made to feel worthless, this book is for you.

Only true individuals shine brightly, be true to yourself.

Thanks as always, Sandra, Bex and Casey for your continued support.

Gez Kelly for proof reading, edits and enthusiasm.

Jenny Ford and Trevor Simpson for reviewing my first draft.

All my friends, too numerous to mention, you know who you are.

Contents

Gender Bender

By

Kevee Lynch

Heels

Sandy Cooper was a normal, middle-aged woman. Normal. What is normal? Who can define normality? If she had been middle-aged back in the sixties, then maybe this might have been true. She was a married mother of two, who stayed at home looking after her family. In this modern age, it's all about getting a career, climbing up the social ladder, employing a nanny to look after the kids, a maid to look after the house, and a gardener to look after the garden and wash the cars. She didn't see anything wrong if people wanted to do things that way. The fact was, she loved what she did. When the kids had been little, she had taken them out every day to the park, or to a zoo, or the library. She loved getting the dressing up box out, or all the paints and crayons, and together they would create masterpieces for her husband Patrick to inspect upon his return from work. Sometimes money was very tight, but as a family they got by. They had friends who had bigger houses and newer cars, but they never saw their kids. Life is a balance. We all want more, but at what cost? She felt happy and contented knowing she had done the best for her family.

Sandy was at home in the kitchen with her daughter, Steph. She was busying herself tidying the kitchen, and Steph was giving her a hand. "Mum, are you coming to watch the boys play rugby this afternoon?" The boys were her brother Joseph, her boyfriend Clark, and their mate Tank, who were all in the living room.

"No, I don't think so. Your dad won't be back from work on time, and he's not playing. And anyway, his ribs are still sore from last week."

"Don't you think Dad's getting a little old for rugby? He's nearly fifty!"

Sandy looked up from what she was doing. "You try telling *him* that. He thinks he's still twenty! He reckons people still play in their sixties. I don't think I can handle him playing for much longer. It takes him all week to recover now. Sundays are the worst. He can hardly move!"

"What's up with men, Mum? They don't seem to want to get old."

Sandy stopped emptying the dishwasher, and a wry smile came over her face. "No one wants to get old Steph, but it's like you turn forty, and the next day you wake up and everything has gone south! If you're a woman, your arse is dragging on the floor, and your boobs are tucked into your belt!"

Steph found this highly amusing. "What about men?"

"Ah well," said Sandy, "they wake up, and they're as bald as a coot, and they can't see their manhood anymore, because their belly no longer fits in their trousers. It just kind of rolls over the top, and hangs down to their knees. They still think they fit into a size 32-inch waistline, and they *do*, it's just that their belly isn't actually in the belt."

"Is that why Dad still wants to play rugby, and you're always at the gym?"

"Well the trouble is, once you stop, there's no going back. Your body's just waiting for you to relax, and then it's like, 'That's it! I'm going to eat and drink and put on loads of weight.' That makes you cranky with yourself, and everyone around you. You have to get up in the middle of the night for a wee, you start saying things like 'back in the old days,' and 'kids these days don't know how lucky they are.' Oh, it's a slippery slope!"

"I can't wait to get old, Mum."

"I don't think it's classed as old these days, Steph. I think it's called middle-age."

Steph loved having a chat with her mum. She was like a mate as well as a mum, a mate you could wind up! "Mum, I suppose you stop having sex, or is that at thirty?"

Sandy came straight back with "Well, me and your father still ..."

Steph butted in quickly. "Alright Mum!" She stood up, clasping her ears. "I don't want to hear it." She headed out of the kitchen, towards where the boys were, in the living room.

Sandy shouted after her "You shouldn't ask if you don't want to hear the answer!" She chuckled under her breath, and remembered, when *she* was younger, also thinking that older people never had sex. It's funny what you think when you're young.

Steph went into the front room to find the boys throwing a rugby ball about. Honestly, you would think they were ten, not nearly twenty! "For god's sake boys, Mum'll kill you lot if she comes in here and catches you with that ball!"

Her brother Joseph pretended to throw the ball at her, which they all found highly amusing. Joseph threw the ball at Tank, who fumbled and dropped it on the floor. As he bent down to pick it up, he glanced out of the window and let out an enthusiastic cry, "Jesus! Look at the booty on that!"

Joseph strolled over. "Oh, it's only Terry."

"Well I wouldn't mind getting behind *that* in the scrum this afternoon!"

This caused eruptions of laughter amongst the other three.

Steph asked "Do you really think so Tank?"

"I *know* so. She's coming in. I'll get the door!"

With that, he ran to get to the door before anyone else. Tank was a lovely fella; a big guy, and ideal for playing prop at rugby. Off the field, he was a gentle giant, but once on it, well, you'd better get out of his way! Like a lot of rugby players, he took the sport very seriously. He considered his fellow-team members his brothers in arms, whether on the pitch, in the clubhouse, or indeed, anywhere and any time that they were together. It's a strange sport to a lot of people, and they have difficulty understanding how you can get drunk with opposing team members, when just forty minutes earlier you were battering hell out of each other. It is hard to explain to people who have never played. Tank just loved anyone connected with rugby. It was a close-knit community, and once you were a part of it, your life never strayed far away from the sport. At this precise moment, however, Tank was more interested in getting to the door, which he did just before Terry had a chance to knock. He flung the door open.

"I'm Tank, a friend of Joseph."

"Oh OK, I'm Terry, an old family friend. Tank, that's an interesting name!"

Tank puffed out his chest a bit, and replied "That's because of my size. I'm built like a tank, you see."

Terry was always up for a bit of flirting, and had a very dry sense of humour. "Mmm, I bet you're packing a big gun as well!"

Tank thought he might be on to a winner here, this Terry was one sassy bit of skirt. "Oh yes" he replied, "this tank is always fully-loaded!"

"I bet you like to get out on a few manoeuvres as well?"

"I'm always up for driving up the gulley."

Terry gave Tank a playful tap on the cheek, and told him to come back in a few years. Tank blushed a little, and watched Terry head towards the kitchen. He went back into the living room. The other three were chuckling away, and then howled with laughter when Tank said "She's a bit of alright for an old'un."

Tank had no idea what was so funny.

"Don't you mean, *he's* alright for an old'un?" asked Steph.

Poor old Tank couldn't quite grasp the situation. "Terry?" asked Clark.

"Yeah, Terry," said Tank. "As in a girl?"

Joseph butted in, "No, Terry, as in my dad's old schoolmate, who's a bloke, you numpty."

Steph rolled on the floor, doubled up with laughter. "Well, that's one to tell the boys at the rugby club this afternoon!"

Terry went into the kitchen and gave Sandy a big hug. They had been friends for a long time. They knew each other through Sandy's husband Patrick, whose friendship with Terry went right back to infant school. The good thing about Patrick and Sandy was that they didn't judge Terry at all. They just loved him for who he was, a kind, generous, loyal friend who just happened to wear dresses! The trouble with society these days was that there were still people trying to tell you what you should and shouldn't do. Society still had antiquated ideas on sexuality.

Years ago, people treated woman as second-class citizens, but thankfully that had mostly changed. People treated foreigners as inferior beings, but in general that had changed too. Disabled people had fought a long, hard battle for rights, and were finally getting results. But the gay and lesbian community still faced daily battles from a wide section of the population. Terry had learned to live with it, and he was able to laugh off the abuse. Or, if the mood took him, he was more than happy to argue the toss with anyone. He knew, however, that Patrick and Sandy just saw him as Terry, the same Terry he had always been.

Sandy took a step back and admired Terry's outfit. "You're looking good today."

"You know me Sandy, I always try my best. By the way, that Tank fella seemed to think I looked good too."

"Hmm," she said, "You're such an old flirt! Do you want a cup of tea?"

"No, no, no," he said quickly, while rummaging through his bag. "Thanks for the offer, but I have to get a bit more shopping done today before I head into London." He pulled out a shoebox from the shopping bag. "I got the shoes."
He passed her the box as she passed him the cup of tea that he hadn't asked for and didn't have time for. He took the tea anyway, slurped some up, and said

excitedly "Open them! You don't know the trouble I had getting them!"

Sandy opened the box to reveal a stunning pair of high-heeled shoes. "Wow, they are perfect!" She held them out in front of her, admiring them.

Steph and the boys all came charging into the room, and Sandy hurriedly tried to put the shoes back in the box. Steph explained that they were all heading off to rugby, but then she noticed the shoes, and made a grab for them. "What have you got there Mum?"

Sandy was a little taken aback. "It's nothing, just a pair of shoes."

Steph pulled the shoes out of the box. "They're lovely Mum!" She turned to Terry. "Did you get me a pair as well, Terry?" She examined them closely, and then a puzzled look came over her face. "I think you've made a mistake here Terry, Mum's not a size nine!"

This caused a bit of a fluster, and Terry grabbed the shoes back. He looked at the size, and then, looking a tad relieved, he explained "You know what I've done? Look, I must've picked up a size nine, thinking it was a size six!" He showed them, a little unconvincingly, holding the shoe the other way, so that it looked like a six.

Tank piped up with "I didn't think they sold women's shoes in a size nine?"

Steph told Tank to have a look at Terry's feet. Terry was a little outraged, saying "I'm only a size eight, I'll have you know!" Sandy ushered them all towards the front door. She'd had enough excitement for one morning.

"OK Mum, we know when we're not wanted," exclaimed Steph.

Terry was still in a playful mood. "Goodbye Mr Tank, nice meeting you."

As they left, Tank turned to Joseph, saying "Well, I never would've believed that!" Joseph just shook his head, while Terry and Sandy burst out laughing.

"That was a close call!" said Terry.

"I know! I didn't know what to say! Do you think they twigged it?", Sandy replied.

"Ha-ha! I don't think so. It's going to be an interesting night, that's for sure! Is he still up for it?"

Sandy sighed, "Yes, I think so, and after a couple of glasses of wine, a little *more* so, I reckon."

"Honestly, Sandy he'll be fine! He's got the legs for it, though I'm not sure he'll be able to walk in those shoes!" With that, Terry walked awkwardly across the room in his heels, pretending to stumble like a man who had never worn high heels before. "What time is he back Sandy?"

"Should be any minute now."

Bigot

Patrick, Sandy's husband, was on his way back home after a hard day's work with his mate Eddie. They were driving along in Eddie's obligatory white Transit van. You know the type, a bit scruffy, with a few dents, and 'This van used to be white,' or 'I wish my wife was this dirty' rubbed into the grime on the rear doors with a finger. That used to be quite funny back in the 80's! Couldn't kids these days come up with anything more amusing?

Patrick gestured to Eddie. "When are you going to clean this van, or did you write that yourself?"

"Fuck off." came the reply, it was the usual response from Eddie. In fact, he used that response rather a lot, to all manner of things. They threw their tools in the back, and started reminiscing about the woman on a former job they had been on.

Eddie was chuckling away. "Do you remember that stuck-up bitch from the big house who never even wanted to say hello to us, you know, the one who thought she was the bloody Queen of Sheba or something? More like Pinocchio, with that hooter she had!"

"Yeah, I remember her. She wasn't nice, was she?"

"Well, she wasn't nice that morning we were working on the driveway, and she had to get out of her car, and she'd definitely upset someone." They were both cracking up now. Eddie was trying to get the key in the ignition, but was laughing so much, he was shaking. "Do you remember, Patrick? Someone had scratched the word 'cunt' into the bonnet of her car. Jesus! She *had* upset someone!"

"I know, and you bloody asked her 'What's that on your bonnet?' She came back with 'I know you builders are thick, but can't you read?' and started to rant on and on."

Eddie was crying by now. "I know, I only asked the question. I mean, who wouldn't ask?"

"I suppose me chipping in with 'whoever wrote that might have a point' didn't really help matters," said Patrick.

"Ha! Not really! I think the only reason we never got run off that job was because she didn't really want to tell her husband why we were taking the piss out of her. Man, that was a funny day!"

The building trade was a laugh a minute, and you never really knew what type of people you were going to be working for.

Patrick then asked "What are you up to tonight, Eddie?"

"You won't believe this. The wife has booked some restaurant in London. Then, we're off to a bloody theatre show! She thinks we don't get out enough together. I'm always out. I'm quite happy going to the local with my mates. She's always welcome to join me, but no, we have to do a bit of 'culture'. What's that all about?"

"Exactly Eddie." Patrick loved to get Eddie going. "The only culture *you* need is beer, darts and football."

"Women always think they know best, but that's what us blokes do, innit? What are you up to tonight?"

"Funny you should ask mate, I'm off to stay the night in London, and take in a show up Soho."

Eddie gave Patrick a wry smile. He knew who Patrick was going with. "Soho? Oh, dear Lord! You're not going out with old gender bender Terry, are you?"

"Gender bender? Jesus, Eddie, no one says that anymore! We're not living in the seventies now, you know!"

Political correctness had somehow eluded Eddie. Back in his day, you said it how you saw it. In the eyes of many, he was a bit of a dinosaur, but in his own eyes, he was simply an unashamedly honest chap. "I can say what I like. I don't think we've voted against free speech in this country, last time I checked. Terry always *was* an odd bloke, and you know it. I stand by what I said. He's a gender bender. Always was, and most likely always will be. End of."

Eddie and Patrick disagreed on a wide range of topics, and it had become almost like a game between them, helping to pass the time on the journey home. Neither of them was frightened to argue the point, and they seldom just agreed to differ.

Patrick pitched in with "He's an individual."

"Yeah yeah, whatever. It's not normal."

Patrick was just pointing out that times had changed, when somebody inadvertently walked out in front of the van. This made Eddie slam on the brakes. He had the window down in a flash, closely followed by a tirade of verbal abuse.

"Are you blind? Can't you see two ton of white metal coming down the road?"

The man was obviously a bit flustered. Not only had he nearly got run over, now someone was shouting abuse at him. "Dreadfully sorry, I didn't see you."

"Didn't see us? You need to get a white stick and a guide dog!" He wound the window back up and drove on. "Bloody twat. Anyway, what were you saying?"

"What I was trying to say, was that times are changing. People are more tolerant to different ways of thinking." Then, he chuckled "It's like you, Eddie. *You're* more tolerant these days too. I mean, you even watch gay porn!"

The van swerved violently as Eddie tried to compose himself. "You're taking the piss, aren't you? When have I ever watched gay porn? Where the hell did you get that from? What a load of bollocks!"

The fact of the matter was that Eddie was not unlike thousands upon thousands of men these days. He was more than happy to kiss his wife goodnight and watch her trudge up to bed, to indulge herself in one of her romantic novels about the poor girl from a dodgy background, getting shagged left right and centre by a bunch of rich company-owning jerks, then for her to find the man of her dreams and exact revenge on the rich jerks, hitting them where it hurts them hardest, in the pocket. That was OK, that was her thing. He preferred nothing better than getting the porn channel on, and watching 'Lesbians Go Wild In Suburbia' and imagining himself in the middle of it all, getting in on the action. That was his fantasy, but it usually just ended in him making a grab for a box of Kleenex. Sometimes he wouldn't get to the Kleenex stage, and would make a dash upstairs to surprise his unsuspecting wife.

Unknown to poor old Eddie, she could hear him coming up the stairs, knowing only full well what he had been watching, and what he was after. So, she would quickly turn off her reading light and be 'fast asleep' when he entered the room. 'Ah, the injustice!' poor Eddie would think. 'What a waste. I should have stayed downstairs!'

Patrick began arguing that watching lesbians was no different to watching gay men, and that it was hypocritical to accept the former, but not the latter. Eddie, however, was having none of it. "What, two blokes kissing? That's disgusting, and you know it! Most normal blokes wouldn't entertain the idea. You've been hanging around with Terry for far too long."

Patrick knew in his heart that Eddie was right. Regardless of how politically correct you were, the majority of men found two blokes kissing in public a little unnerving. He wouldn't admit this to Eddie, though. Not a chance. He wouldn't want to fuel his fire. He put it down to their age. Back in the day, when they were kids, it just didn't happen. It certainly wasn't on the television, you wouldn't be taught about it at school, and if your dad had caught you kissing another bloke, you probably wouldn't have lived to tell the tale. But attitudes change and evolve over time, and the younger generation were, in general, much better-informed and tolerant. Homophobia was the last bastion of a bygone age, but Patrick believed that another twenty years should put paid to it. "It's our age group Eddie, we're dinosaurs."

"I don't want to discuss it anymore. I know Terry's a mate, but it's still wrong. End of."

The rest of the ride back to Patrick's house was quiet, apart from the odd expletive coming out of Eddie's mouth as he raced the Transit through queues of traffic, dodging from lane to lane. Patrick thought it better to say nothing, and just grin and bear it. He knew that if he asked Eddie to slow down, he would simply floor it all the more.

As they rounded the corner into Patrick's road, who should be just coming out of Patrick's house? Terry. You couldn't have written the script any better. Terry was just giving Sandy a kiss goodbye, and telling her not to worry about tonight, and that it would be great fun. Patrick leaned over and started tooting the horn as they approached.

"Pack it in Patrick!" shouted Eddie, annoyed that Patrick was invading his space. They pulled up to the house, and Patrick jumped out to greet Terry and Sandy. Terry gave Patrick a big hug, and noticing that Eddie was watching, also gave Patrick's arse a big squeeze, kissing him on the cheek, too. Eddie wasn't amused, and shook his head, muttering to himself under his breath.

Terry knew that he could always make Eddie feel uncomfortable, and called over to him "Come here Eddie and give me a hug, don't be shy!"

Eddie, in his usual sarcastic tone, remarked, "Nice dress, Terry. Is it one of your mum's?"

"No, darling, I borrowed it from your wife."

"Hey, fuck off and don't take the piss. How's your dad by the way, has he got over your choice of fashion yet?"

"Nice try Eddie, but you're not going to wind me up today, I'm in a great mood!"

Eddie knew that if you mentioned Terry's dad, it would usually get him riled. Terry's dad was a real salt of the earth builder, who had never got over his son wearing dresses, and what father would? Eddie was on a roll, and kept on. "I hear you're taking Patrick out tonight. Mind he doesn't get accosted by one of your bender mates."

"Are you worried, Eddie? Did you want to save Patrick for yourself? You can come with us if you like, keep an eye on him."

'My god', thought Patrick, 'don't these two ever stop?' Once upon a time they had been great mates. At school, they were always together, and it was hard to figure out what went wrong. Had Eddie just been sucked into the macho habit of attacking everything you didn't understand? 'Let's not change the status quo'. That seemed to be order of the day for a lot of people in our society. You simply cannot be different.

Terry and Eddie were still arguing, with Terry sarcastically reminding Eddie of the times he used to stay at his house after school, for a sleep over. "Come on Eddie, I'll show you mine, if you show me yours, just like the old days."

Poor old Eddie turned bright red. He really didn't need reminding of such things. He shouted to Sandy that he was off, and crunched the van into reverse. It was all getting a bit much for him, and he backed inf to a lamppost.

Terry could be quite cruel sometimes. He had the ability to cut people down and make them look stupid. It was like a defence mechanism, after all the years of abuse he had suffered. He had learnt that most people who dished out abuse could not take it at all, and that they usually had some dark secret to hide. "Do you remember, Eddie, when we used to practice smooching, for when we pulled the birds? Come on, let's have a dance now!"

"Just piss off, you gaylord!" Eddie slammed the van into gear, and screeched off down the road.

Terry laughed as he got into his car. "What a jerk!"

Sandy commented "Well, you *do* have to wind him up!"

"I think he winds himself up. Anyway, enough of that. I'll see you tonight. And Patrick, thanks so much for tonight. It really means a lot to me."

As Terry drove off, Patrick was feeling a little anxious. He turned to Sandy, and was about to say something. But she already knew what he was going to say. They had been together an awfully long time, and she could read him like a book. "You can't let him down, Patrick, you promised." Patrick knew he had promised, but he had been drunk at the time. They walked into the kitchen. "All the kids have gone to rugby. Are you going down to watch?"

Patrick was somewhat surprised by this question. "Are you joking? The lads might ask me what I am up to tonight. What am I going to say? Oh, I'm off to Soho with Sandy and Terry for the night. You've got to be joking! I've had enough already, with Eddie taking the piss."

Sandy wasn't surprised. "Honestly, you guys. You all have to be so macho! You don't want to show you have a feminine side. And the funny thing is, *most* of you have a feminine side."

Patrick walked over towards the sideboard. "Do you fancy a gin and tonic?"

"Yeah, why not? I think you'd better make yours a large one. You might need it!"

She walked towards him, and stroked the side of his head. "It'll be alright." She clinked glasses with him.

"Cheers." They both took a swig.

"I *am* a little apprehensive," said Patrick.

"I know you are, darling, but it'll be fine. I'm looking forward to it."

They embraced, and the look on his face said it all. He'd faced plenty of challenges in his life, and done lots of different things, but was he ready for tonight? Only time would tell.

Eddie and Chloe

Eddie was pondering things, as he often did on his drive home. He liked to think he had done rather well in life. He had a nice big house, big car, plenty of disposable income, a wife, and of course three children, who had all done well and moved away. They did come to visit sometimes, but he felt it was mainly to see their mum. Was he a good parent? He liked to think so. Alright, he may not have been around as much as he would have liked, but he had to work. Work had always been his number one priority. Without work, you didn't make money, and he liked money. Even going to the pub was work. Think how many jobs he had picked up in the boozer! His father had always worked hard, but had nothing to show for it. That's why Eddie had always wanted to work for himself. The more work you did, the more you earned for yourself, not some boss.

He loved doing jobs with Patrick now and again. Patrick was a great tradesman, but a crap businessman. He could have been worth as much as Eddie, but he seemed to spend it quicker than he earned it. He thought about how different they were. Eddie's plan was to work hard, secure his future, then retire at sixty-five, and start taking a few holidays, safe in the knowledge that if he lived to a hundred, money wouldn't be a problem. His children could then divide up his estate when he was gone.

He remembered when he had been working with Patrick some years back, building some walls, which needed to be finished over the weekend. The guy they were working for had said "Name your price to get it done Saturday, and I will pay you it." Before Eddie could speak, Patrick had said they couldn't come in, as they had another job booked in. Yes, they had, but it was a fifty quid each job, a favour to an old girl. Eddie remembered the argument well. He had to let Patrick have his way, and they earned fifty quid instead of a possible hundred and fifty. When they returned on Monday to the other job, someone else had come in at the weekend and completed the walls. The work done was of a poor standard, and got condemned. Patrick and Eddie not only got paid to finish the job, but to take down the other work first. Nevertheless, it had been a turning point in their working careers, as Patrick wanted to ease off on weekend working and spend more time at home, while Eddie wanted to take on more and more work, and so they drifted apart for a bit. Patrick's take on life was that if he reached sixty-five, he would be pleased. He didn't want to be lying on his death bed thinking 'I didn't do this', or 'I didn't do that.'

Although he would never admit it to Patrick, now that they were getting towards later life, there were actually a few things he wished he had done, like maybe a few more holidays with the family, rather than staying behind to finish a job. Now his family was at the stage where they did their own thing, and it was just himself and Chloe. He was going to put his dislike of the theatre to the back of his mind, and try and enjoy himself tonight. Yes, give the other half a good night out, still sink a few beers, but embrace the culture.

Chloe was getting herself ready for the big night out with her husband. She had been to the beauty parlour.

Hair, nails, exfoliation, massage and face pack. The new dress and shoes were all ready to go. And the new coat. Well, why not treat yourself? The cleaner had the house looking tip-top, and had even prepared a spot of light lunch to keep them going until supper. Eddie's suit was back from the dry-cleaners, along with his shirt. Yes, she was ahead of schedule.

She loved Eddie, there was no doubt about that, and she had learned to adapt to his way of thinking. She wanted for nothing; Eddie had seen to that. He was a shrewd man where business was concerned, and had managed to secure them a comfortable lifestyle. She knew how to work him. If she had a good idea about something, she needed to make him believe it was *his* idea, and then it would happen. She'd started going out a bit more in recent years, now that the kids had flown the nest. She would like to see more of the kids, but they had all moved out of the area. Was it because Eddie was a bit overpowering, maybe? She was somewhat surprised that he had agreed to go to the theatre tonight. Surprised, but pleased that at last he might be mellowing. She enjoyed her life and the things she had, but something was lacking. It was always niggling away at the back of her mind. It was Eddie. He just wasn't exciting.

When they were younger, and starting to date, he used to shower her with presents and take her out all the time. He always insisted on paying; he was old-school. They had then knuckled down and bought a house, followed by kids, and all Eddie wanted to do was work. She was grateful that he had provided well for the family, but what had happened to him? These days, she spent most of her evenings immersed in a book, reading other people's fantasies. There had been a time when Eddie would come round to take her out, and he would be all smiles, smartly-dressed, and smelling nice. He couldn't wait to embrace her, pay her compliments, and later, try and get into her knickers. These days all that was a far, distant memory. Now he just came home, ate his dinner, and was off to the pub. The only time he got amorous was after ten pints and a kebab, and quite frankly that wasn't really doing it for her.

She looked at herself in the mirror, and considered what she saw before her. She had kept herself in shape, but her eyes showed no evident spark, no reflection of the excitement of a life that had long since gone. She still wore sexy lingerie, but it was for herself rather than for Eddie. He would always pass out before getting to that part of undressing. Speaking of underwear, she didn't really want to see Eddie's. He still wore the same type of underwear he used to wear when she first met him. Y-fronts. Who the bloody hell invented them? It must have been a priest or something, back in the sixteenth century. Now, she wasn't stupid; the thought of Eddie in a thong, with his beer belly hanging over the top was something no one would ever want to see. But a pair of boxers, or anything a bit different would help. What was it with blokes? No one can see what they are wearing under their jeans, but they are all too frightened to be a bit risqué, in case they get run over and have to go to hospital. She didn't know what she wanted, really. Perhaps a good night out with her husband was just the tonic she was after. He'd be out of his comfort zone, so he might lay off the booze a bit. Yep, maybe a shag would be on the cards for tonight. Who knows, she might even get on top of him, give him a bit of a surprise!

Soho

Terry was in a hotel room in Soho. This area of London was like a second home to him. He had contemplated living here many times during his life. He loved it here; you could be who you wanted to be, and nobody batted an eyelid. OK, so you got the odd stag do ending up around here late at night, intrigued to know what Soho was all about, but that was usually just out-of-town people being curious, or on occasion wanting to give a bit of abuse. The chances were that among these groups of men, two or three of them would be struggling with their sexuality, but too frightened to come out, or to try something different and expand their horizons.

Terry loved his life. He had seen attitudes towards him change over the years. It wasn't perfect, but the younger generation were definitely more open-minded about things. The Internet had played a huge part in bringing together people who previously may have felt on their own. You can be made to feel an out and out minority in this world, but technology had changed that forever. As much as he loved Soho, he still loved being out in the countryside, though, where he had grown up. He may have moved a few miles away to get away from family and acquaintances, to somewhere he was unknown, but fundamentally he hadn't travelled far.

Terry was very slight, with a figure most women would die for. Everything Terry wore was meticulously selected. He believed that in order to look sexy and appealing, you had to truly believe that you were. From underwear to coat and hat, every layer had to complement the previous layer. Stockings were a staple part of Terry's wardrobe. Let's face it, no great look ever started with a pair of baggy jogging bottoms. A nice tight-fitting black dress, barely covering the top of the stockings, was always a winner. It had to be just long enough to keep people guessing if they were tights or not. High-heeled shoes were a must, and he'd perfected the art of walking in them a long time ago.

When you start wearing heels, it's like learning to drive a car. At first you are all over the place, too slow, stumbling and stalling, with everyone laughing at you. Terry believed that walking round the living room for hour upon hour in his mum's oversized heels had given him a head-start. He also liked a wig, the sort that would make people look at you. Sophisticated but sensual. And the make-up had to be just-so. Not every now and again, but always. Joan Collins would never go out without a full face and wig on. Maybe they should get out together, the Terry and Joanie tag team. Now, *that* was a thought!

Terry always reckoned that he had a major advantage over women when it came to guys. The fact that he was born a guy, albeit a feminine one, meant he knew what guys liked and wanted. And a conservative, mousey look wasn't it. Yep, Terry was a stunner, to men and women alike! Everybody loved to look at Terry!

And so the big night had arrived, and Patrick and Sandy would be here soon. The excitement was all getting a bit much for Terry, and he just hoped it would go well, and that Patrick and Sandy would enjoy it. He opened the door to his room. He thought he'd better check that they'd got there, and to his surprise, they were just arriving. He looked at his watch and shouted to them, "Its 7pm! What are you doing! We have to be at the club by 9pm sharp!"

Patrick gave him a confused glare. "That means we've got two hours! I only need twenty minutes to get ready." Terry looked horrified! Who on earth could get ready in twenty minutes? Patrick continued "Terry, I have been thinking, maybe this isn't such a good..."

Sandy gave him a dig in the ribs. "Don't worry Terry, he'll be ready." She opened the door to their room, and shoved Patrick in. She closed the door behind them, and they looked at each other and giggled. They'd had a couple of drinks to get themselves going. Maybe a couple too many.

Sandy put the suitcase on the bed and unzipped it. Patrick headed to the bathroom, turning and muttering "I'll take a shower then." She nodded in agreement, and flung open the case. She hung a couple of items up, then turned on the TV with the remote, finding a dance music channel, and pumped up the volume, thinking that would get them in the mood.

"Right. Shoes.", she said out loud to herself. She pulled out the new high heels. "You're going to love these!" Then she started pulling other items out. Two thongs, two sets of stockings, and a blonde wig for one pile. "I'm going to love this!" A couple of bras, and a massive bag of make-up.

Patrick came out of the shower, singing, then clocked the outfits on the bed. He looked at Sandy pensively, fear and dread coming over him. "I just don't know, Sandy. I don't know if I can do this." He stood there with a towel wrapped round his waist, drying his hair half-heartedly with another.

She cupped his cheeks, shook her head a bit, and tried to give him a little encouragement. "Patrick, we've been together a long time, haven't we? How many times have you slipped my panties and stockings on in the bedroom, and we've had some fun? Do you think no married man ever has slipped into his wife's underwear? Because if you think that, you are very deluded." She gave him the big wide-eyed look, the one that demanded an answer.

Patrick casually picked up a bra. "I've never worn one of *these.*" He replaced it, and picked up the wig. "*Or* one of these." Then he stared at the shoes, picked them up, and exclaimed "And how the *hell* am I going to walk in these!" He studied the shoes further. "Jesus, they're even my size!"

Sandy pointed to the wardrobe, where two dresses were hanging up. Patrick looked. "I don't know, it's one thing doing a bit of role-play in your own bedroom, but the full ensemble? What if somebody I know sees me? I'd be a laughing stock back home!"

"Oh Patrick," she said soothingly, "don't be a wuss. Who'd recognise you anyway? Which mates of yours apart from Terry ever come to Soho? You *know* it is a big night for Terry. I think the 'Date A Straight Mate

Night' is an excellent idea, encouraging people to come out of their comfort zone. Or closet. All Terry's mates are getting involved, so you certainly won't be the only cross-dresser virgin in the hall! Come on, man up. Or should I say 'woman up', and get on with it!" She was losing the soothing tone, and starting to push him a bit. "Besides, you might even enjoy it!"

"I might not, though."

"Look, get yourself dressed, and I'll sort your make-up for you after my shower. You OK with that?" He sort of nodded.

He hunted out the mini-bar, located a small bottle of vodka, looked in the mirror and toasted himself, with a quick wink. 'Ah well, in for a penny in for a pound!' He pumped up the volume further on the television, dropped his towel, and selected a thong, thinking 'This is a good place to start.' It kind of fitted OK, so he pulled on the stockings one by one, being very careful not to ladder them. He'd done that a few times for his wife, when it was her wearing the stockings. Next the suspender belt, which proved a little bit tricky, but he managed to get it done up. Then the bra. Now, he'd *definitely* never got *this* far before. He struggled to get it done up, giving in and spinning the clasp to the front, then spinning it back. It was padded, and made him look like he had a chest.

He looked down. It was time for the dreaded shoes. 'Hmm, they slip on easily enough. Perfect fit.' Looking down at the shoes and stockings, he thought he looked pretty good. Now for the big stand. He pushed himself up and grabbed onto the wardrobe.

Sandy came out of the bathroom just as he was trying to take his first step. He toppled forward, but she managed to catch him. "You should have waited, Patrick. you could have hurt yourself!" She pushed him back up and gave him a little squeeze. "What's this Patrick? Bit of a semi-lob on? You been getting excited trying your new gear on, eh?"

He was a bit flushed, not sure if it was because he was aroused or because he'd nearly broken his ankle. She knelt down and gave his ankle a rub, then started stroking it a bit, and his calf. She was teasing him and he knew it, trying to make him relax, and take his mind off the evening ahead. The trouble was, he really *was* starting to get side-tracked. A quick flick of the finger from Sandy put paid to any more thoughts along those lines.

"Oy, that hurt that did!"

"Later, if you're capable. We need to crack on with the rest of your outfit, and mine. I'm not being upstaged by my husband."

She led him round the room a bit in his shoes. He did quite well, having always had good natural balance. She let go, walked around behind him, and gave him a slap on the butt. "Your butt is better than mine."

He looked in the mirror. "Not bad, eh?"

"Hmm, come on, let's finish you off ... no, you fool, I meant your make-up."

She turned the music up even more, and they continued getting dressed. Patrick slipped into his tight-fitting little black number. It certainly hid a multitude of things. Sandy sat him down on the bed, and started applying make-up to his face. After a while, she said "Your face is sucking a lot of this in. Your skin is so dry and cracked. I thought I told you to start moisturising last week?"

"Do you not think Eddie might have noticed if I'd turned up with soft skin? It was bad enough shaving my legs and chest and concealing *that*. He *did* make a comment about me not wearing shorts. I always wear shorts to work."

"You *do* know your son and all his mates moisturise, and shave their chests, don't you? Probably half the blokes you work with do too. Sometimes you're more like Eddie than you think." Patrick chose to ignore this comment, as he knew she was after a response.

Sandy was getting chatty now, as she busied herself around him. "Perhaps you should have brought your trowel with you. You could have put this on yourself!"

"Ha-ha," he mumbled.

"I was reading in the paper last week, a survey on men wearing women's underwear, and the results were quite high. It was a secret online survey. I wonder what the results would have been like if they carried out the survey at the local pub?"

Patrick had an answer for this one. "It would all depend on the time of night. From 7pm-9pm, no one would admit it. From 9pm -11pm, you might get the odd 'I've tried it'. 11pm-1am, once the old alcohol has set in, most blokes would be saying 'yes'. Some might even be bragging that they were wearing some there and then. Everything tends to get a bit exaggerated after a few pints."

"Yes, I agree with that! Most blokes would be telling you how big their knob is after a few drinks, only for the wife to be putting her hand up and wiggling a little finger."

Patrick thought this hilarious. "That's like a scientific discovery you have hit on there, Sandy. Drink affects males and females in two very contrasting ways. We think things get bigger, and women know things get smaller." It was a sad but true fact, and they both fell about the place laughing. A thought suddenly occurred to Patrick. "Getting back to women's clothes, I couldn't imagine Eddie slipping into a pair of Chloe's pants. Where would he tuck that beer belly?"

"He'd have to get a pair of control pants, wouldn't he?"

"I tell you what I think, he'd have to get a scaffold tower to pull that lot together! That is one bloke who shouldn't wear his missus's clothes!"

"You don't think even Eddie might look sexy?"

The illusion wasn't working for Patrick. "Not a chance! For one thing, he'd have to smile. That doesn't really happen too often."

Sandy finished the make-up, and popped the wig onto Patrick's head. A few minor adjustments, and she looked pleased with the result. "Right, close your eyes, stand up, and I'll point you towards the mirror. OK, what do you think?"

He opened his eyes. "Well well, I don't believe it. I look nothing like me."

She passed him a clutch bag. "You'll need this for your things."

'Why on earth would I need a bag?' he thought. "I might have my period, is that it? Don't I need some of those little mouse things?"

"Don't be vulgar," came the stern reply. "You need this for make-up, a purse and your phone." She passed him the items, and said "Right, we're good to go."

A quick knock-knock on the door, and Terry barged in. Good job they were not up to anything, having left the door unlocked. Terry was quite flabbergasted. "Look at you! I never ever thought I would see the day. You scrub up pretty well! Fabulous job, Sandy! Right, where's my phone? I need a picture of this."

Patrick didn't want any of that. "No, Terry, please. I don't want any photos. I don't think I could explain this one to the kids. I'm sure they wouldn't mind, but the lads at the rugby club might have a few words to say."

Terry understood Patrick's apprehension. It took a lot of guts to do what he was doing. Mind you, being in Soho, it wasn't so bad. If Patrick had taken the train into town, he may well have experienced a whole new world. The old saying 'you can't judge a book by its cover' doesn't always ring true, in a lot of people's minds. He turned to Sandy and gave her a good look up and down. "You look absolutely gorgeous, my love. Well, let's see if London is ready for us three." He took them both by the hand. "Let's get this party started!"

They headed out towards the lift. Terry pressed the button, and they waited. Patrick was certainly feeling a bit uneasy, with a look of impending doom on his face. He was hoping they didn't bump into anyone on the way to the club. That would be a good start.

The bell rang, and the lift door opened. To Patrick's horror, there was already a couple in the lift. Sandy took Patrick's hand, and led him in. It was very quiet, and the groups exchanged the obligatory nod of the head. Was this bloke staring at Patrick? He certainly was eyeing up all three of them. The woman he was with, possibly his wife, was glaring at him, knowing full well that his eyes were roving. After what seemed an eternity to Patrick, which was really only about thirty seconds, they reached the ground floor, and the door opened. The couple emerged first, with the woman mumbling under her breath about him checking everyone out. He looked a bit sheepish as she frog-marched him out of the hotel.

Terry, Sandy and Patrick all looked at each other and started laughing. Sandy had a bit of a giggling fit, then said "Oh my god, Patrick! He was *so* checking you out!"

Terry stepped back and took a look at Patrick's legs. "He certainly has got the legs Sandy."

Patrick didn't know if he was amused or worried, and gestured towards the bar. "I think a drink before we walk down the road. The bar looks fairly empty, thank God."

A drink was definitely in order. They linked arms, and headed into the bar.

Eddie's big night out

Eddie considered himself to be a top bloke. He had provided well for his family, was a popular person in the local community, and well-known in the local pubs. He liked the status quo. You went to work, and charged people as much as you could get away with. You visited the local pub as often as possible, and maybe took a holiday now and again. Oh, and changed the car every three years. That was Eddie pretty much mapped out. This format had worked well for the last thirty years, so why change it? He was a contented man, yes, but he still liked to moan about the country and everyone in it.

So, taking the wife out once a year up London to the theatre was no big deal, really. He would never admit it, but he was glad to have Chloe with him. He was out of his comfort zone in The Big Smoke. Just too many people rushing about, too many beggars asking for money, and generally oddballs all over the place. Yep, once a year was plenty. They had been to a fancy restaurant earlier. He didn't mind splashing the cash around once a year. He wasn't into your fancy wines, though; a pint of bitter was his drink of choice.

Chloe loved the city, and often came into town with her friends. She was always a bit apprehensive about taking Eddie, but going out like this once a year as husband and wife was surely the right thing to do? It gave her something to add to the conversation when she was lunching with the ladies. She genuinely loved Eddie, and she always remembered her sweet mother telling her "Never try and change a man, Chloe. Some women assume, when they meet a man, that they will be able to change him when they get married. No chance. If they like the pub with their mates now, they always will." She'd had her eyes wide open when she married Eddie, and sure enough, he had never changed.

She missed her children, but understood that they had their own lives to lead. She secretly yearned for them to pop round more often to see their Dad. He was strict, and he might seem uncaring, but that was just his way.

Tonight of all nights, a big night out in London, and Eddie had *still* managed to get to the local before getting the taxi. She had spent all day getting ready so that he wouldn't get the opportunity, but oh no! Eddie had showered and dressed in a flash. "I'm just popping to the local for a quick one!" he had exclaimed. When has a man ever popped to the pub for one drink? It doesn't happen. The taxi arrived, and she had to pick him up en route. Not the best start to the evening.

Then the restaurant. She should have known not to book a French restaurant, but she had thought a steak would do the trick. Trying to get a steak the way he wanted it, well-done with no sauce, had proved a problem, however. And only French mustard! No beer, except lager in bottles. It had been a laugh a minute!

The best thing about being out with Eddie on her own was that she could be herself. Not one of the ladies who lunch, just Chloe, out on the piss with her old man, like thirty years ago. Where had that time gone? It only seemed like yesterday that she, Eddie, Patrick and

Sandy were getting pissed together, putting the world to rights.

She missed Sandy. They had drifted apart a bit over the years. Sandy wasn't one to do lunch. She was always doing her own thing, mostly with her family. They would have to get together soon for a night out. It always ended up messy when they got together!

So, the meal hadn't gone well. The theatre, on the other hand, had been a total disaster. What was she thinking? Billy Elliot, a good working-class hero story, that's what. She hadn't told Eddie what they were going to see, which in hindsight might have been an error of judgement. He wasn't going to watch a load of blokes prancing about dressed as ballerinas! No, that wasn't going to happen. She had managed to persuade him to reluctantly give it a go, but after twenty minutes, and him not returning from the toilet, she found him in the theatre bar. He had told her to go back and watch it, but she wasn't that bothered. She just wanted to be with Eddie.

They left the theatre and went for a stroll, found a nice pub with real ale and a good gin selection, and got on it. Four pints in an hour had Eddie in good form, and the gin was slipping down well. They even had a bit of a snog in the corner.

Chloe decided that Eddie needed a bit of a walk to control his alcohol intake. They headed off hand in hand, walking the streets of London, looking for another bar. It had turned out a good night so far, and it wasn't even 9pm yet.

Hotel Bar

After the lift incident, Patrick certainly needed a drink. He had thought this was going to be hard, but it was proving harder than he could have imagined. Terry was first to the bar. "Six tequila slammers please, bar tender." He turned to Patrick. "Trust me, this will help you walk better in those shoes. I know. I was once where you are now."

Sandy nodded her approval. "When did you actually start wearing women's clothes, Terry?"

"Patrick will back me up on this. It was when we were at primary school. We used to have a big dressing up box. I suppose we were about six at the time, in Miss Price's class." He took his tequila, as did the others, and they each slammed both shots down. "Another round please, sir."

Patrick looked a little more relaxed now. Perhaps the earlier drinks were kicking in, or maybe he wasn't feeling so conscious of his attire. "I remember it well. All the boys and girls used to get dressed up. Poor old Terry was a bit slow, and always used to get to the box last. There were a lot more women's clothes than men's, so Terry always got the short straw."

"Well, I never used to rush, did I?"

"What, you did it on purpose?" asked Patrick.

Sandy in a sarcastic tone, said "Duh! ... Yes!"

After all these years, it suddenly dawned on Patrick. "Jeez, am I thick, or what?"

Terry was in talking mode now, and once he was off, it was difficult to stop him. "Do you remember when we were sixteen? My dad made me work for him during school holidays? He didn't want me going to Art School, and thought a few weeks with his company would sort me out."

"Yes, I remember it well. You only lasted a couple of weeks."

"All these years and I have never told you why, have I?"

Patrick was trying to think back, but it was a long time ago. "You said you had a row with your dad over something, he gave you a clout and told you to leave, and you moved away to your auntie's house."

Terry downed another shot., "That's not quite the full story. I went to work, it was freezing cold, my skin started to dry out, and my hands got all rough. The two bricklayers Dad had put me with said rather than getting long-johns to wear underneath my trousers to keep warm, I should do what they did, and wear a pair of your wife's tights. 'Think about it,' they said, 'women walk around in tights all day, and don't get cold, so if you wear a pair and put your trousers over the top, you're warm as toast, and the trousers stop the tights from laddering. No one knows you have them on. It's great!'"

"Yeah," said Patrick, "I had a couple of bricklayers say the very same to me, I thought it was a wind up, and bought some long-johns."

Sandy was intrigued to see where this story was going, and asked Terry "So, what happened?"

"I went in to work the next day, we're all in the tea hut, and they're asking 'Have you got your wife's tights on?' and I'm like 'Yes, well, not my wife's, as I haven't got one, but my Mum's.' So they ask me to show them, I drop my trousers, and at that precise moment my dad walks in the tea hut. The bricklayers are on the floor laughing, Dad's like 'What the fuck?', clouts me round the head, and tells me to fuck off home. Dad gets home later, shouting and screaming at me, says I've embarrassed him, and he's had to let two good bricklayers go, because he doesn't want rumours spreading. That was it. I said I would move away. I didn't want another clout. And that was the extent of my short-lived building experience."

Sandy couldn't believe it. "All for wearing a pair of tights?"

Terry gestures for them all to take another shot. "Sandy, you know me, darling, I wouldn't be seen dead in a pair of tights!" He took another shot. "I had a pair of my mum's stockings on, complete with a suspender belt and a pair of lacy panties!"

Patrick, who was just downing a drink, spat it out all over the bar. "Jesus, Terry! No wonder your Dad hit the roof!"

Sandy thought that was just brilliant, and Terry continued "The only tights my Mum had were flesh-tone, with control pants in them. Me, in flesh-tone tights? Darling, that simply wasn't going to happen."

"Eddie might have worn them," said Patrick in a sarcastic tone.

"Let's not go there," said Sandy, "That's another story."

Patrick decided to get off the bar stool, and nearly fell over. He'd forgotten he had high-heeled shoes on, but luckily Terry caught him. "It's time to start acting like a lady. Are we all set?"

They thanked the barman, linked arms, and headed towards the door, starting to sing a Black-Eyed Peas song. "I've got a feeling ... that tonight's gonna be a good night ... that tonight's gonna be a good good night."

They reached the door, opened it, and practically fell into the street.

Sometimes when you go out for the night, you never know how things are going to turn out. Most times when you think it will be a good night, it isn't. If you're not looking forward it, then it'll often be a blinder. Tonight was one of those that could go either way. Terry was looking forward to it, as was Sandy. Patrick had started out dreading it, but things weren't going too badly. Split seconds can make a massive difference to a night out. You might just miss the train, and arrive an hour late. You may just miss a taxi, and you can't get home. The most unpredictable thing about a night out is that you never know who you might bump into.

The split second that Terry, Sandy and Patrick fell out through the door, was the same split second that Eddie and Chloe were walking past. The chances were millions to one, especially as Eddie had never set foot in Soho before. He wouldn't be here now, only Chloe had made him walk miles in search of a bar. He wasn't even aware that they had strayed into Soho.

As they bounced into each other, Patrick sobered up instantly. He clocked who it was, put his head down, and headed straight back into the bar. This wasn't good. One minute he had been getting into the spirit of things, finally relaxing, and the next minute the big bad wolf had appeared, and this night was going pear-shaped. What had he been thinking, dressing up like this? He should have known someone would see him. You can't even walk to the shop these days without getting caught on a thousand cameras. He could see it now on 'You've Been Framed,' a section on trans people, and a focus on him, staggering down the road in high heels. He ordered another drink, and put his head in his hands. 'What an idiot! Why did I do this?'

Outside, Eddie was surprised to see Sandy. "Hello! Crikey, you lot have had a skinful!"

Terry gave Chloe a big cuddle, and turned to Eddie. "You look like you have had a few yourself!"

Chloe was quite excited to see Terry and Sandy. "I don't believe it! Fancy meeting you here! What are the chances?"

Sandy couldn't believe it either, and although she was excited to see them, she knew Patrick wouldn't be. "I thought you were off to a show tonight?"

"Yeah, well, here's the story, we *did* go, but Eddie wasn't very happy about it. The truth is, I booked tickets to Billy Elliot. He lasted ... well, not long at all really. Said he didn't want to sit through blokes prancing about doing ballet. We left, headed to a bar, then I thought we'd better take a stroll, as Eddie was drinking at his usual lightning pace."

Eddie didn't think he was drinking any quicker than normal. In fact, all this walking had got his thirst up again. "I'm ready for another! The thought of the ballet, and men prancing about in tights has turned my stomach a bit. No offence, Terry."

"Terry wouldn't be seen dead in tights, would you Terry?"

"No Sandy, that's for sure!"

Chloe gave Terry a good looking over. "I think you always look nice Terry. No, actually, stunning. You always look stunning."

Eddie was somewhat unimpressed. "Each to their own." Chloe looked daggers at Eddie. "You look nice, Terry. Is everybody happy now?"

A brief silence ensued. Eddie started to look around. "Where's Patrick?

Sandy masked a sigh of relief. It appeared that Eddie hadn't twigged yet. "He's just coming. I think he was settling the bar bill."

"Righto, that dishy blonde bird might be keeping him company at the bar. Come to think of it, who was she? Nice set of pins! I wouldn't mind!"

He got a dig in the ribs from Chloe. "You're not out with your pub mates now, Eddie, living in your fantasy world of women fancying you. Fine catch, you and your mates would be! You're too old, and you'd run a mile if she gave you the come on."

This was a strange situation. Sandy tried to figure out her next move. "She's just a friend. A bit shy. I'll go see if I can find her." She headed back into the bar, leaving Terry, Eddie and Chloe to make small talk.

"It's a nice place, this Soho," said Chloe, "I've never been before, seems very lively."

"You wait until later! This is nothing, there's hardly anybody out yet."

Eddie was scanning the area, not quite so impressed. It was the first time he had ever seen blokes walking down the street holding hands. "I'm not so sure we'll be staying that long, will we Chloe? We have a few things to do."

Chloe knew Eddie had been relaxed and enjoying himself for the last hour, but now he was clamming up. "I'm not going anywhere until I've seen Patrick. He should be here in a minute. Then who knows? Get Terry to take us to a club. What do you think Terry?"

Terry took everybody as he found them. Having suffered a lot of bullshit in his life, he had vowed never to judge anyone. How Eddie would fit in at the club was an interesting question. But he couldn't see Eddie taking too well to Patrick dressed as a woman. "I'm heading to a club, not sure it will be Eddie's cup of tea, but you never know. Unfortunately, it's not a Radio 2 playlist Eddie. The music might be a bit too happy for you."

In the bar, Sandy came up behind Patrick and gave him a cuddle. There was a multitude of shots and beers lined up in front of him. He took a big swig from a pint. "I just had a feeling, Sandy, that something would happen tonight. This is a situation I could've done without."

Sandy was thinking the same, but was it really that bad? It wasn't as if he was trying to hide anything, and he was doing a mate a favour. "Answer me this, Patrick. Eddie and Terry are your two best mates. You work with Eddie, true, but how often do we see him out of work? When we were skint, when the kids were young, it was Terry who helped us out. When your Mum was ill, and we were away, who looked after her? He's looked after the kids, taken me shopping. Now, I know Eddie would do the same, but it's Terry who's always done it. He's never asked *us* for *any*thing in his life. It's easy for me to say, as I'm not the one cross-dressing, but if he asked me, I would put a suit on and grow a beard."

This made Patrick chuckle. "I'd rather you didn't try and grow a beard. I know your mum has one."

She tickled him, to stop him there. She cupped his face with her hands. "Terry is your best mate, and mine. You said you would do this, and I want you to do this. I'm enjoying you doing this. I'll prove that to you later. Pull yourself together, don't worry about what anyone else thinks, do what you want to do." She took a drink, and the speech was over, apart from "I promise you some fireworks later, when we get back here." She gave him a little kiss.

His expression changed, as though the weight of the world had just lifted off his shoulders. "You're right. Fuck it!" He looked down at his shoes, "I'm quite enjoying wearing these, you know."

"As long as you don't start wearing mine!"

"Call them in, I need a hand with all these drinks. I can't *wait* to see Eddie's face."
Sandy headed out to get the others.

The barman looked at Patrick. "You're doing a good thing for your mate. You're a *real* mate, remember that."

With that, the others came into the bar. Patrick had his back to them, a little frightened to turn round. Sandy passed them some drinks, a slammer and a beer each. They all knocked the slammer back, and Eddie also took a swig of his beer. Sandy did an introduction. "For one night only, I would like you to meet the other Patrick."

Patrick stood up, and turned around. Eddie's eyes caught his face, and he spurted his beer out all over the bar and the barman. Terry tried to brush the beer off the barman, but the barman didn't care. He was loving the floor show. Chloe was nearly speechless herself, but came out with "Patrick! Well I never! You look good! Very good! Better than me!"

Eddie wasn't quite getting the same vibe. "Oh, my giddy aunt! What are you thinking? The lads are going to love this on Monday!" Eddie's face had a beaming smile, while Patrick's was fading somewhat. "How are you going to live this one down, Pat, me old mate?"

He took another swig of his beer. Chloe was getting agitated with him now. "Eddie, just shut it. You won't be mentioning this to anyone."

"You have *got* to be joking! I'll be living off this for years to come! What a fucking story!"

"What about you Eddie? said Chloe. "I still have that Polaroid of you prancing about in a pair of control tights, from when we first started going out."

"It was a joke. The lads at work told me to try them on, for the cold work."

"That's as maybe, but you didn't have to keep them on at your mum's house, dancing round to Queen, thinking you were Freddie Mercury, did you?"

Eddie was looking a bit sheepish now. "Have you really still got that photo? I thought you'd thrown that away a long time ago."

Terry handed Chloe a flyer about the 'Date A Straight Mate' night. He explained that the night was just about enjoying yourself, and getting a glimpse of something different. She had a read, then addressed Eddie. "Right. We're going to this tonight, no ifs no buts. I won't make you dress up, although I *would* like to see it." She looked him up and down, then turned turns to the others and said "No, I don't think I would, actually!"

They all laughed, apart from Eddie, who was still wondering about that Polaroid photo. The barman gave them a round of drinks on the house, thinking to himself how much he loved his job, and how he couldn't wait to get to the club later, to see how Eddie was getting on.

The Club

Normally when you head to a club, you try to look a lot more sober than you actually are. Bouncers can be terribly picky about who they let in. Sometimes it's not simply a question of 'Your name's not down, you're not coming in'. It might be 'Your face doesn't fit, you're not coming in.' Bouncers know that some groups are trouble. You have to have that feel about you in this job. Terry knew the bouncers, so it wasn't going to be a problem getting in. If Eddie and Chloe came on their own, it might have been a bit different. Not because they were drunk, or dressed a bit too conservatively for Soho. It would have been more that Eddie had an uptight face, and through no fault of his own, his miserableness might offend others, so they may have got moved on. It's not an exact science.

We have all stood in that queue, thinking 'I won't I get in.' Eddie remembered when he was a 'good boy' at school, and they made you sit up straight and cross your arms, and they would let you go one at a time. No matter how hard he tried to sit still, with arms folded, he never got picked first. He was usually one of the last, though he never knew why. Was it a vindictive teacher who didn't like him? This was why he didn't like clubs, because it was out of your control as to whether you got in. It was up to the bouncer, and the more Eddie tried to look relaxed, the worse it would be.

It was an unusually busy night, especially at this time. Was it because a lot of the people attending would normally be at home watching a bit of Saturday night television? The advance publicity for the night had been good, judging by the number of people. There were people from all walks of life, different cultures, different social standings, and different sexual persuasions. Some people had turned up out of curiosity, and others, like Patrick, were doing something they wouldn't normally do. With gay clubs, you knew what music you would be getting; loud, banging house music, with a cheesy classic or two thrown into the mix.

Terry bowled straight up to the front, ignoring the queue. He greeted the bouncer with a kiss, and signalled 'five' with his hand. The bouncer ushered them through, much to the annoyance of the people at the front of the queue. A glance from another bouncer soon quietened the complainers. Eddie was at the back, keeping his head down. Out of the five, he was the most conservatively dressed. The bouncer grabbed his arm as he passed. "I'm not going to have any trouble with you, am I?" It was more of an instruction than a question.

Terry took Eddie's other arm. "Ha! No, I'll look after him." He dragged Eddie along, which Eddie found highly amusing.

They walked into the main club area, and ... Wow! The place was banging! Not only could you hear the music, but you could feel it vibrating through your bones. The crowd was mixed, and there seemed to be a lot of rather uncomfortable-looking blokes dressed up in women's clothes. They headed over to the bar area, which was a bit quieter. Terry gestured to the barman, with his hand again indicating 'five.' The barman nodded, and the drinks were on their way. It was a long time since Patrick and Sandy had been to a club, and Sandy was already feeling the music. Eddie and Chloe had never been in a club like this; Chloe was feeling it, but Eddie wasn't quite 'in the zone' yet.

Terry greeted a couple of his transsexual mates, and started talking to them. He gestured to the others to come over and chat, and introduced Patrick. "Sabrina, Bob, meet one of my oldest friends, Patrick."

Sabrina checked Patrick out. "Looking good, Patrick. What do you think, Bob?"

"Hello darling. Patrick, you are a natural. Are you sure you haven't been before? Look at that butt, that *is* impressive! Check this out, Sabrina!" Bob turned Patrick around, so they could admire his rear end.

"You're right, Bob, that *is* nice!" Sabrina gave it a little squeeze, and an approving pat.

Sandy was enjoying all the attention that Patrick was getting. It was true that he had a good shape on him. Perhaps he should wear a dress all the time, she thought!

Terry pulled Eddie over. "And this is Eddie, and that's his wife Chloe, and Sandy, who's Patrick's other half."

Eddie didn't receive the same admiring views that Patrick had. In fact, Sabrina seemed a little unimpressed with his conservative dress sense. "You didn't fancy getting dressed up Eddie? Never mind, perhaps next time me, Bob and Terry could work a bit of magic on you, sharpen you up a bit."

Terry gave Eddie a little rub on the cheek. It was obvious that he was outside his comfort zone. This most definitely wasn't the local pub. Terry enjoyed watching him squirm a bit, though. "Oh, he's just a little shy. Doesn't get out much in The Smoke. Perhaps he needs a bit of a dance, to loosen him up a bit."

"A bit shy, are we?" Sabrina took one of his arms, and Bob took the other. "What do you reckon, Bob? Can we get his motor running on the dance floor?"

Bob was up for it, but Eddie wasn't having it, and sort of wriggled free. "No, I'm alright, ladies. Erm ... do I call you ladies? I was just going to get another pint." The Ladies looked at each other, decided that this was not an option, and without another word grabbed his arms again and headed out towards the dance floor with him.

Chloe shouted some gleeful encouragement. "Go on, Eddie! Don't be a jerk! Enjoy yourself for once!" She turned to the others. "I've *got* to get some photos of this!" Then she was off after them, and smiling away. She knew full well that Eddie fancied himself as a bit of a dancer, and with all that drink inside him, who knew what might happen? Whatever *was* about to happen, she wanted a photographic memory of it.

Terry, Sandy and Patrick headed back to the bar. The barman already had some drinks lined up for them. He leaned over the bar, and gave Terry a kiss on the lips.

"Good effort tonight, with your friends. Well done, Terry."

"I'm as surprised as *you* are, especially with *that* one." Terry pointed over to Eddie, dancing. "Now *that*, is a fish out of water." He put his arm around Patrick. "Thank you for coming. It means the world to me."

Sandy cuddled in with Patrick and Terry. 'What a lovely night out,' she thought. "I was just thinking; I'm out with my two best mates, and I'm getting outshone by both of you. Mind you, I have a chance to be the better dancer, because I can't see Patrick getting round the dance floor in those shoes very well."

Terry had the answer to this, and started making shapes with his hands. "Big fish, little fish, cardboard box. Keep your feet still, throw a few shapes with your hands, and move your head. House music. You can blag the dancing, even if you're shit. Most people in here are hammered on drink or drugs, and don't pay much attention to anyone else."

They stood by the bar drinking, throwing a few shapes, and generally having a fantastic time. Eddie and Chloe were somewhere on the dancefloor, getting down with Sabrina and Bob. Conversation, as always when slightly inebriated, was all over the place. Sandy, with a slight slur in her voice, said "Terry, I want to know, who did you really fancy when we were all younger? Not necessarily someone you know, but an idol, maybe. Patrick has a really weird one, don't you, Patrick?"

"You *love* bringing this up Sandy! I was a young, adolescent boy, and we are entitled to fancy whoever we want."

"Tell Terry! Come on, don't be shy!"

Terry was intrigued. It wasn't something he had ever talked about with Patrick. Perhaps they hadn't talked about it because Patrick didn't want to know what turned Terry on.

"Alright, alright! I'll do it." He looked Terry in the eye. "When I was younger, I had a bit of a thing for ..."

He paused for a second, but Sandy finished his sentence for him. "Lady Penelope off Thunderbirds! He had a massive crush on Lady Penelope!" She jumped up and down, clutching Terry's hands. "A fucking puppet fetish!" Sandy could let rip with the odd swear word when she got excited after a few drinks. She wasn't being nasty, she just found it hilarious that her husband fancied a puppet.

"So what? I'm admitting it! In them days, she looked very lifelike to me. A beautiful, classy lady!"

"She was a puppet! With strings! Terry, tell him it was a bit odd."

Patrick was laughing at himself, and yes, looking back, it may have been a bit strange. "Didn't you find Joe 90 attractive, Sandy?"

"No, I didn't! He was a puppet! Terry, tell him he's odd. And, tell us who *your* first crush was."

"I have to be honest, and tell you I didn't really fancy anyone at that age. I wasn't sure where I was at, but I *did* idolise someone, and wanted to be like them."

Sandy was desperate to know. "Who was it, then? Come on, the suspense is killing me!"

"Well, I wanted to look and act like ... Lady Penelope." Sandy couldn't believe what she was hearing! She was having a laughing fit.

Patrick was surprised. "How funny is that? I never knew! Come to think about it, we both really loved Thunderbirds and watched it in our early teens, often together."

Sandy was on a roll. "Unbelievable! You both had a puppet fetish, and neither of you knew! Patrick, *you* were probably masturbating, dreaming of shagging her, and Terry, *you* were probably getting excited about the little two-piece she had on. This is why I love you two so much! You're so similar, but so different! Didn't you ever fancy anyone real, you know, like a person, Terry?"

"Yes, sort of ... I mean, as I got older. I really wanted to be Barbarella. Those costumes were unbelievable."

"I can't believe you two! Patrick loves her as well, but "hello chaps", she's a character played by Jane Fonda, she's not real! You two live in cloud-cuckoo land!"

"Control your wife, Patrick, she's getting a bit lairy. So, after all these years, our secrets are out. How can two mates not know this about each other?"

Patrick thought the same. "I know, it's odd. And the funniest thing is, the first real woman we both loved and admired is right beside us."

"I'm with you on that as well, Patrick. She used to dress sexy, still does. Big hair and big eyes, you have to have the big eyes, and a heart of gold."

Sandy was enjoying the compliments from her two best mates. "So, I'm expected to say 'thanks' for being compared to a fucking puppet and a Sci-fi character, am I? Well, I will, because I loved them two as well. Let's get pissed and find Eddie and give him some stick. Although I think he probably had a hard-on for Margaret Thatcher when he was younger."

Eddie was having the time of his life. He started off with the old dad-dancing, but then the drink kicked in, and he had now entered a wondrous fantasy world. Bob and Sabrina were extremely beautiful, and boy, could they move on the dance floor! Eddie thought he was in the middle of a couple of supermodels! His inhibitions had sashayed out of the building, and those two getting up close was just the tonic he needed.

Chloe loved seeing Eddie this way. He was usually so guarded and self-conscious. She knew the drink had got the better of him, but in a good way. Unlike the normal Eddie, which was ten pints in the pub, then home to moan. What fun they could have if he was like this all the time! The reality was that she'd better make the most of it, because it was unlikely to happen again for a very long time. Chloe was no slouch on the dance floor herself, and was now enjoying some attention from Eddie, as Sabrina and Bob had moved on. Eddie embraced her, and clenched her buttocks. He really was out of character.

"Chloe, now I don't often say this, but I *do* love you. I know I'm a bit of an arse sometimes, but I'm going to get better. Spend more time with you, starting from tonight." Chloe thought that was lovely, but she kind of shrugged it off, because she knew that what he was trying to say was 'any chance of a shag tonight, if I'm capable?' She actually *was* up for it, the reality being she would struggle to get him to the bedroom, he would probably go and throw up in the en-suite, half wash it off, insist on making love, not be up to it, get the hump with himself, and go to sleep. He would then wake up in the morning with a banging headache, and no recollection of anything that happened after about 8.30pm. He might even sheepishly ask the question 'Did we have sex last night?' But at this moment in time, things were good. Maybe she could get him to walk a few miles. It might sober him up.

The others caught up with Chloe and Eddie, along with Sabrina and Bob, and all seven had a great night, drinking, laughing and dancing. Eddie had a fantastic night, dancing with anyone who happened to come within two feet of him. Chloe was like David Bailey. She must have taken 500 photos, mostly of Eddie. Patrick did well, but had to ditch the high heels for a bit, when he was involved in a dance-off to a bit of RUN DMC.

Sandy spent most of the night drinking, laughing at Eddie, and trying to work out if Patrick was enjoying his new attire a little too much. Terry was having a ball! Although he and Eddie didn't see eye to eye on most things in life, they *did* go back a long way, and if push came to shove, he was sure Eddie would help him out. He was thinking how great it was to see Eddie enjoying himself, the reality being that Eddie would be back to his old self tomorrow, with tonight's antics wiped from his mind forever.

Sandy and Chloe decided it was time to get the lads home. It was 3am, and Terry was only just getting started, but they and the lads were dead on their feet. They said goodbye to Terry, and agreed to catch up at Sandy and Patrick's house tomorrow.

Getting out of the club and hitting the fresh air didn't seem to improve Patrick and Eddie's state of intoxication. The girls were pretty smashed as well. What a night! They strolled down the street, and it wasn't looking good! Eddie and Patrick were hand in hand, swaying all over the place. Patrick's walking in high heels had improved a bit, though his drunken swaying nearly cancelled this out. Eddie occasionally broke into a little dance, shouting out "Stack the shelves! Shopping trolley! Cardboard box! Little fish!", the dance moves he probably wouldn't remember in the morning, already getting them mixed up with each other, and out of order.

They reached the hotel, and Sandy turned to Chloe. "Do you want to stay with us tonight? We could sneak you into our room, and the lads could sleep on the floor."

Chloe didn't think so. "Look at the state of them. You'd think they were eighteen. I'd better walk him around for a bit. If he goes inside anywhere now, he'll be as sick as a dog. Eddie, say goodbye to lover boy! We need to let them get to bed."

"Ok, sure. Haven't we got time for one more drink, darling?"

"No, come on, let's be having you."

Eddie, in his drunken stupor, whispered in Patrick's ear. "You hear that, buddy? That's code for 'I want to get you on my own for a big sex session.'" They both looked at Chloe, and he whispered again "You can see it in her eyes. She wants it bad! I better go. Good luck buddy, I'll see you in the morning." Patrick embraced Eddie. Another unusual gesture, as it was usually a handshake at arm's length, using one hand only.

Off they popped, leaving Sandy with the unenviable task of getting Patrick up to the room. The movement of the lift might not be the best idea, so they decided to go up the stairs. The shoes were proving a bit difficult now. "Take them off, Patrick."

"I will not! I've got this far!"

They struggled onwards, reaching the top, where Patrick fell flat on his face. Sandy helped him up, but couldn't help laughing and getting the giggles. They made it safely through their room door without further incident. She left him standing beside the bed. "I need the loo. Get undressed."

Patrick was very drunk, speaking very slowly and precisely. "No. I am keeping my shoes on. Me and my shoes, my shoes and I, have become one. And we are ready for a night of wild passion."

"Oh, OK." She closed the bathroom door.

Patrick looked at himself in the full-length mirror. He pulled his wig off, then his dress, then his bra. He stood admiring himself in the mirror, with just his heels, stockings, suspenders and thong. He talked to himself in the mirror. "Patrick, you are the best-looking bricklayer in Soho." He let himself fall backwards onto the bed, shoes dangling over the edge.

Sandy came back into the bedroom, thinking that he did indeed look quite sexy. She popped back to the bathroom, calling out "I'm just taking a bit of make-up off. I have it caked on tonight, and I don't want any spots. *You* could do with taking some off too, Patrick. I can't believe you've got a bit of a lob on. I thought you'd be spark out." She entered the room, flung off her dress, and turned the light off. She was still talking as she got onto the bed, beside him. "I'm so looking forward to this. Does this mean we are a bit weird? I suppose what we do when we are alone is our own business. Prepare to be excited, I'm coming in!"

She started kissing his neck, and slid her hand down, caressing his leg. She liked the feel of the stockings. She moved her hand up slowly, then realised that nothing was going on downstairs any more. She looked up. He was spark out. She gave him a couple of nudges, in the hope of waking him, but to no avail. She gently kissed him on the forehead, and whispered "I love you. Goodnight, Patrick."

The Morning After The Night Before

Is there a worse feeling than the morning after the night before? Sandy was driving Patrick home, and he was struggling. They had both had a skinful last night, but she was bright and breezy, and wasn't really feeling it at all. Patrick had fallen straight asleep, whereas Sandy had drunk about three pints of water and read a book. It had been a quiet journey home, with Patrick nodding off every now and then, and when he was awake, it looked like he was in deep thought.

They pulled onto the drive, and not a minute too soon. Patrick wanted to say something. "About last night. I don't think the kids need to know too much about it. Let's keep it on a 'need to know' basis."

"Your secret is safe with me, lover boy, although there's not much to tell."

They got out of the car, and Patrick was feeling a little sorry for himself. "Alright, I know I fell asleep. That wasn't the plan, I can assure you. I *may* have got a little carried away. I was under a bit of pressure last night."

They were just about to put the key in the door when it opened. Joseph popped out first. "Hi, clubbers! Me and Steph are just on our way out, you can tell me all about it later. C'mon Steph, hurry up!"

Steph came rushing out. "Oh hello, you two, how did you get on? Good night?"

Joseph was getting impatient. "We got to go, Steph."

"I'm coming! Gotta go, Mum and Dad." She gave them each a kiss. She started staring at her dad. "What's that on your eyes, Dad? Is that eye shadow?"

This flustered Patrick somewhat. "What? Eye what?" He rubbed his eyes.

Steph rubbed at his eyes too. "It is! You've got eye shadow on! Mum, look at Dad's eyes!"

Sandy had a look, and she too gave them a rub. "Oh, it was from the club, last night."

Patrick suddenly felt empty inside, and could only murmur "Sandy ..."

Steph was completely confused. "What, you mean it *is* eye shadow?"

Sometimes you have to think on your feet. Patrick wasn't saying a lot, but Sandy had it covered. "An 80's theme night Steph."

"Oh, new romantics, Adam Ant that sort of thing? For a minute, I thought you were turning into Terry, Dad!"

"What do you mean, Steph?" asked Patrick, still a little confused.

"Nothing really. You know I love Terry, but I couldn't imagine you in a pair of high heels." Laughing as she spoke. She started to walk away, but shouted to her mum. "You should have kept those shoes for Dad! They might have fitted him! Ha-ha! See you later!"

She got in the car with Joseph, and you could see her telling him the story, laughing all the time. Sandy and Patrick went into the house, and closed the door. Patrick let out a massive sigh. "That was close! Think I got away with that one! All in all, it was a good night, though."

"Well, don't forget you have Eddie coming round in a bit. Once he gets you to work, he'll want to *slaughter* you in front of the lads. You're not in the clear yet!" They headed into the kitchen, and Sandy put the kettle on. "Nice cup of tea will sort you out. Don't worry about Eddie; what will be, will be. Just admit to what you did. It's no big deal."

It might not be a big deal to Sandy, but she didn't have to put up with Eddie all day long. Still, the job was nearly finished, and he had his own work to start soon. The doorbell rang, and Patrick went to answer it. He took a deep breath, and opened the door. Eddie and Chloe. Who else would it be?

Eddie was straight into him. "Ooh, hello Sailor, mind if we climb aboard?" He pushed past Patrick, and went to greet Sandy. "Morning Sandy, have you got a kiss for a *real* man?" He was in a surprisingly good mood, very perky, considering the amount of drink he had consumed.

Chloe followed in. "Don't mind that twat, Patrick, he has been like this all morning. It's doing my head in.

You look a bit the worse for wear though." Patrick half managed a grin, hoping they were just dropping off some stuff, and then hopefully they would be on their way.

Sandy was intrigued to know how they'd got on after they left them; Eddie hadn't been looking too good. "How did your evening pan out, Chloe?"

"You may well ask! We ended up walking to Kings Cross. He was being sick all over the place! I'm surprised he remembers anything."

"I think I must have ate something a bit dodgy in that French restaurant. Or someone slipped something in my drink. It's all a bit of a blur, really, apart from that black dress and high heels Patrick was wearing! Nice outfit, Patrick, never realised you had joined the gender bender brigade! I can't wait till we get to work, to tell the lads. You won't need a tool bag for you trowel, you can put it in your handbag."

Eddie laughed at his own jokes, but nobody else could be bothered with him. Chloe was distracted by the laptop on the side, and asked if she could use it for a minute. Sandy passed it to her, and carried on making a cup of tea for everyone.

Patrick remembered something that Chloe had mentioned last night. "Did you manage to fish out that Polaroid of Eddie in his control tights? I think I'm going to need that at work tomorrow, as a safeguard, to shut him up."

Before Chloe could say anything, Eddie, who now had a smug look on his face, said "She won't be able to find that. I found that years ago, and destroyed it. I couldn't risk that ever seeing the light of day."

"Have you been through my things?"

"I had to! That photograph could have been damaging to me! What if one of the kids found it, or you divorced me, or worse still, you told my friends about it? I had to cover myself. To be a success in this world, you have to cover your tracks. Politicians do it all the time."

It wasn't what Patrick wanted to hear. He slumped a bit in his chair, thought about it for a while, then said "You know what? I don't care. *You* were at the club as well, last night, enjoying yourself, I seem to remember. How are you going to explain that one?"

"Being at the club is one thing, ... " he was distracted, as music started coming out of the laptop. "As I was saying, being at the club is one thing, but being dressed like *you* at the club, is a different kettle of fish."

Chloe turned the laptop round, so they could all see. "And *dancing* at the club with a couple of transsexuals is a bloody great pondful of fish!"

A video was playing of Eddie sandwiched between Sabrina and Bob, gyrating away, with Eddie grinding up on Bob's backside, shouting at the camera "This is fucking amazing!"

"Good old Chloe!" exclaimed Patrick. It looked like she had saved the day. "Loads of photos, and a great video, too!"

"Call it security, Patrick. You can always upload it to You Tube if you like. I can see that one going viral!" She beckoned to Eddie. "Come on, John Travolta, time to go. Sandy, we'll pass on the tea, thanks. Come on Eddie, stop looking so pathetic. It's only a video. You have to say, though, it's quite funny!"

Eddie's mood had changed very quickly, and he was ready to make a hasty exit. "Right. Yes. Let's go. Patrick, don't worry me old mate, your dress-wearing secret is safe with me." Sandy and Patrick saw them out, waved them off, and went back to the kitchen.

What a morning! Patrick had been through the mill emotionally, as had Eddie. Chloe and Sandy were more level-headed, and sometimes they couldn't understand their respective partners. Men always had to be so macho, never let the guard slip. Why worry what others think of you? Do whatever you want, or whatever makes you happy.

The video was still playing. Chloe had in fact caught them all on video. Apart from Eddie and his new-found friends, Patrick, Sandy and Terry could be seen throwing a few shapes. "I don't look too bad, actually, do I Sandy?" asked Patrick.

"I still fancy you, with or without your shoes!" She gave him a kiss. "Come on, let's go upstairs, and finish what we started last night."

They headed out of the kitchen, like a couple of school kids on their first date. She rushed back and grabbed the laptop. "I don't think you want to let the kids find this video. Not yet, anyway."

They rushed upstairs, but then Patrick turned and rushed back to the kitchen. Sandy went into the bedroom and turned the volume up on the laptop, the dance music from the video still pounding out. Patrick came in, and pulled his high heels out of a bag. They smiled at each other. Patrick closed the door.

Is It A Beautiful Game?

By

Kevee Lynch

Egos over here, and egos over there

Kids' football is a wonderful thing, or so you might think. Dedicated coaches and parents encouraging the children to embrace fair play, act as a team and help each other out. Winning is important, but isn't the be all and end all. It's taking part that matters. Very noble thoughts, and while the powers that be that run all sports would have you think that this is what happens every weekend, the reality is sometimes very different.

Coaches' egos can get in the way of such an ethos; they want the success on their CV. Over-protective parents can get all angst-ridden on the touchlines, and if another player dares to tackle their child, the cries of 'foul!' and 'send him off, ref!' ring out. These parents played thirty years ago, club legends in their own memories, now trying to re-live their former glories, or perhaps re-invent the past, and do so through the kids' team. Some of the kids are actually not all that interested, but play anyway, at the insistence of their parents or the coach, who hope that their own reputations might be enhanced.

Also on the touchlines, you get the normal folk with a healthy attitude, the ones who are simply happy to see their children enjoying themselves. If their child wants to give it up and try something else, that's fine. It's great to play football, rugby or netball on a Sunday morning, but if you fancy swimming or learning the piano, it's not the end of the world, is it?

Seamus, or 'Sha' as everyone called him, was a dad whose eleven-year old son played football. Sha was thirty-eight years old, and he had a bit of a different look about him to most of the other dads. His hair was plaited, his clothes were baggy, kind of 'surfing-dude' style, and he always drove around in his beloved VW camper van.

He was just walking over to where his son was due to play football, a bit late, having had to pop into work to finish a couple of things off. As he approached the pitch, he noticed it was the A-team playing. His son played in the B-team so he hadn't missed the start.

The coach, Eddie, and his assistant Dave were shouting towards the pitch. 'Nothing unusual there' thought Sha. Sha wasn't really a shouter, and he certainly didn't shout anything negative.

The coach did, however, and was just now shouting at one of the boys, Greg. "Greg, what are you doing?" Greg looked over and shrugged his shoulders. He knew better than to answer back to Eddie. "If you can't kick the ball, kick the man!", Eddie continued.

"I tried," offered Greg, but he needn't have bothered.

"Well you ain't trying hard enough!"

Eddie then started on another lad. "Ron, get stuck in! Don't let anyone run past you like that!" He turned to Dave. "Did you see that Dave?"

"Oh yes," Dave had seen it alright, and was also eager to add his bit. "He's taking the Mickey out of you son. Sort it out!" Eddie put his hands around his head in such a display of anguish that you might have thought he was an actor.

Sha walked over and stood next to Eddie, his hands in his pockets and looking out onto the pitch. He asked "How's it going, Eddie?"

"How's it going? How's it going? I'll tell you how it's going, we are a load of rubbish! I've never seen us play this bad. This team we are playing is bottom of the league. Bottom of the bloody league."

'Oh well, you ask a question, you get a reply,' thought Sha. This was bad though, Little Olney never lost. Well, not the A-team, anyway. "What's the score then, Eddie?"

"The score? What's the score?" Eddie often answered your question with another question. "We are winning two-nil, but it's a disgrace! A bloody disgrace! I've never seen us play this bad!"

Just as he said that, the other team scored, eliciting an anguished and angry cry from some of the Little Olney crowd of "Referee!"

The ref looked at his watch, blew the final whistle, and that was it. Game over.

Dave began to remonstrate. "Ref, he was miles offside. You can't award that goal!" He ran onto the pitch, closely followed by Eddie. Well, it was more of a walking shuffle, really, as they were both a bit out of shape.

Seeing them approaching, the ref put his hand up as if to say 'Don't come any closer.' "The lad wasn't offside. I have made my decision, the goal stands, and the game is over. I would be grateful if you would leave me alone, thanks."

As if that was going to happen! Eddie was first to actually reach the referee, and he put his face right in the official's. "Who's paying you, ref?"

The ref had heard it all before. He started to feel annoyed, but managed to stay calm. "The goal stands. The result is 2-1. It hasn't affected you winning the game, so now will you please get out of my face so we can get on with the next game, or I shall report you to the Football Association."

Eddie threw his hands up theatrically, and Dave did the same. Eddie shouted over to the B-team. "Right you lot, get warmed up quickly. A-team ... over here. Sit down, and shut up."

Another dad, Mark, was keen to offer advice. "You'll have to tell them, Eddie, that was crap!"

Mark didn't have to tell Eddie what he already knew. In fact, what would Mark know? He had never played football in his life. Eddie really could do without his unwanted input.

Dave was allowed to offer up his thoughts, though. "Our one hundred percent record of no goals conceded, gone. What were you thinking?"

The goalkeeper, Adrian, was quick to point out that it wasn't down to him. "It was offside."

"No it wasn't," said Dave.

"But you said to the ref ..."

Eddie cut him short. "It doesn't matter what we shouted at the ref, the lad was miles onside. I've told you lot before, get in the ref's face. It doesn't matter if he is right, just put the doubt in his mind."

Sha butted in, "Eddie, the B-game is about to kick off, and the boys want to know what positions you want them to play in."

Eddie was doing his de-brief, and didn't like to be interrupted. "I'll be over in a minute. I need to sort this lot out first. It doesn't matter who starts where. The result will be the same."

Sha walked over to the B-team, a bit bemused by Eddie's attitude, and beckoned them all together. "Right, Eddie will be here in a sec. What are your starting positions?"

The boys looked at each other blankly, and some just shrugged their shoulders. One of the lads, Robbo, spoke up. "We don't really have starting positions. It changes every week, and if we go a goal down, it all changes again."

Sha's son, Freddie, also spoke up. "If you got here a bit more often to watch, you'd know that, Dad."

Sha knew his son was right. He had been working so hard that he had let their father/son time slip somewhat. That was about to change. He had promised himself he wasn't going to work any more weekends. The more money he earned the more he spent, anyway. "I know son. Things are changing from today, though, I promise." Then he addressed the team as a whole. "Come on then, who wants to play where? Play where you feel comfortable. Who usually subs?"

"We don't have any," said Robbo. "They always go with the A-team."

That didn't surprise Sha very much. "Come on, heads up lads, you've got the chance to play where you want, so just go out there and enjoy yourselves. That's what you're here for, isn't it?" The lads all nodded in agreement, and got themselves sorted and ready for the kick off.

The ref blew the whistle, and the match began. By their own usual standards, it was a good start. Five minutes into the game, and they hadn't let a goal in yet, and they looked to be enjoying the game.

Sadly that changed as soon as Eddie and Dave came bounding over. Eddie started shouting from the moment he reached the touchline. "Robbo, what the bloody hell are you doing? Get up front! Jono, defence. Steve, mark a man!"

The lads got confused trying to change positions, and inevitably, their opponents scored. "You lot are bloody useless! How can you call yourselves a football team? I'm wasting my time with you lot, I really am!"

The game continued, but Robbo suffered an injury, and had to come off. Now playing with a man down, and with Eddie's constant reshuffling, the team lost five-nil. Eddie could only offer up his usual barrage. "Rubbish! Absolutely toilet! I've never seen such a disgrace. Get out of my sight, the lot of you."

The boys trudged off, looking dejected. None of the parents dared say anything to Eddie. Sha was made of different stuff, however, and being unhappy with Eddie and his attitude, said "I think you were a bit harsh on the boys, Eddie."

Eddie was not at all used to people questioning him. "Harsh on them? After a performance like that, Sha? I know the soft, politically-correct brigade might agree with you, but this is real life, man. You have to tell them now, harden them up for the future. Harsh on them? You got to be kidding me! Do you know what, Sha, I have pretty much had it up to here with the B-team. If you think you can do better, why don't you take the job?"

"Eddie, you know I know nothing about football, I'd be about as useful as a handbrake on a canoe."

'You're not wrong there,' thought Eddie. "It's all very well coming over shouting the odds, but you're not man enough to take on the job. Useless. Just like that team. No backbone. Do you want the job, or not?"

Sha felt backed into a corner, one which was difficult to get out of. He was about to make a decision that he would probably regret. His wife would find it amusing; his son might not, but he heard himself saying "Alright Eddie. I'm in."

"Training starts Wednesday at six pm. Don't be late."

Eddie walked off, chuckling away to Dave. Freddie, who had heard it all, was very surprised. It would be great to see more of his dad, but his dad was by no stretch of the imagination a football genius. And he was too soft to manage a football team.
Breakfast

On Monday morning, Sha was sitting in his kitchen drinking a cup of tea. His beautiful wife Sarah was busying herself getting breakfast ready. She was thirty-eight years old, and in Sha's eyes, she was as beautiful now as the day they had met. She was his rock, and always had been. Whatever mad-brain scheme he came up with, she always supported him one hundred percent. However, she was struggling a bit with his new venture into football management. She knew Sha better than anyone, and she knew he could take things to heart, and she was worried that this might turn out to be an emotional roller-coaster ride too far.

"Sha, football manager, seriously? Do you even like football that much?"

He could see her point, he really wasn't that fussed about football these days, and could take it or leave it. As a kid though, he'd loved it, especially going to games with his Dad. He even used to take his son Freddie, but the swearing and aggression had just got too much for him. It was only a game after all.

"Good point, but Eddie doesn't want to do it anymore, and I kind of backed myself into a corner."

"Sha you don't like the swearing at the kids or the ref, but that's what happens every week. I'm not sure why Freddie likes going." She paused as she walked out of the kitchen, and shouted up to Freddie. "Your breakfast is ready Freddie." She came back in, saying to Sha "Another thing Sha, you're too nice. I really don't think it's for you."

Sha wasn't sure what she meant. "How can you be too nice?"

"Other people just want to win at any cost. You're not like that. OK, I know you like to win, but you won't want to win by any means possible. Face it, you're a bit of a softy, and that's why I love you. I don't want you changing on me."

Sha however, reckoned he'd learned a lot in his thirty-eight years about what makes people tick. "I know there are aggressive people around, but that doesn't mean that I'm going to become one."

Sarah brought the plates over to the table, and smiled sarcastically. "You might turn into one of those football hooligans!"

This had Sha howling with laughter. "I can see it now on the news, riots at Little Olney under twelves' football match. Sarah, I think *you're* the one that needs protecting. It's a simple coaching role, it can't be that hard."

"You can't take anything seriously can you? It's like having another child!"

As Sarah bent down to get the sauce out of the cupboard, Sha jumped up, grabbed her from behind and pulled her onto his pelvis. "I don't know what you mean I'm always serious."

Just then, Freddie walked into the kitchen, "Dad what are you doing, you're sick! Leave Mum alone!"

Sha sat back down. Sarah looked a bit flustered. Sha ruffled Freddie's hair, saying "Nothing sick about loving your Mum."

Sarah got Freddie his breakfast, and asked "What do you think of the new manager?"

"Well, he won't shout as much, and he's *watched* a lot of football. We can't lose any more than we already do, so technically he won't be any worse than the last manager. Only time will tell Mum."

Sha got up and headed to the toilet, feeling chuffed that his son had given him a vote of confidence.
Sarah was pleased really. It would do them both good to spend more time together. "He'll be alright son. He'll

always try his hardest, you know how he is if he puts his mind to something."

"I know Mum."

"Your team are a pretty nice bunch."

"I'm not worrying about *my* team, it's the boys from the other teams and their parents that might be the problem."

She put her hands around his head, then gave him a big kiss and a cuddle. "How's it going at school? It's a big step up to secondary school."

"It's OK, Mum. I liked my old school and friends better. At least I still see my old friends at football. Some of the bigger boys aren't so nice, and a lot of people seem to get into fights."

She felt for him, because big schools could be a bit daunting. "I remember being at big school with your dad, and he hated it. He used to get picked on quite a bit because he looked a bit different."

"Dad's not afraid of anyone, Mum."

"He isn't, but when boys are four years older than you, and take a dislike to you, it can be hard. The thing with your dad is that he's never afraid to give you his opinion. Which is great, but sometimes it's handy to keep your mouth shut."
"Dad always says to hit back."

"Yes, your dad *would* say that. He thinks if you hit back, they might leave you alone. That doesn't always happen, though. He's a lover, not a fighter. We need to look after him. Will you do that at football for me?"

"Course, Mum." They hugged, then Freddie shouted "Bye Dad, love you!" and headed off to School.

Sha came back into the room. "Oh, he's gone. Was he OK?"

"Yeah, fine. Bit like you, though. Feels a bit trapped. Most things you do, you can stop. If you don't like football, you can give it up. If you don't like going on trips, you don't have to. Even when you get older, if you don't like a job, you can leave. But you can't just leave school, you have to go, and changing school isn't easy. Like I said, like you, he feels a bit trapped. What time's my brother picking you up? Half the day's gone."

"About ten minutes ago!"

"Why are you helping him out? You don't need to work anymore. The money coming in from your book is plenty for us, you're doing the house, and now you're managing a football team as well. Do you need the stress of working with my brother?"

"I know all that, I just feel I'm not ready for the scrap heap yet. It does get me out and about a bit, and let's be honest, your brother is a bit disorganised when it comes to work. He works hard but he hasn't quite got it."

He got up to give her a cuddle. He was feeling a bit romantic this morning. A horn beeped outside, which meant that his lift had arrived. He kissed her goodbye, and she shouted after him as he left "Have you got your lunch?"

"I'm working with your brother," he shouted back. "I have a suspicion we will be hitting a café. See you later!"

Car

Sha jumped into the van, Neil having got out to let him in. It was the standard Transit, three seats across in the front, and you usually put the smallest person in the middle. Wayne, Sarah's brother, was driving. Wayne and his friend Neil were both thirty-three, and had been friends since school. Both of them liked a drink and a smoke, both liked to moan a lot, and both liked to take the piss out of Sha. Sha didn't mind; he sort of expected it, and if they were taking the piss out of him, at least they weren't moaning. It was like they had rehearsed this morning's greeting, chuckling away in unison "Morning, Sven," Sven being a reference to a former England football manager.

News certainly travelled fast around these parts, one of the joys of living in a village. Wayne continued "It's major news around Little Olney this morning! I couldn't believe it. You, a football coach! God help those poor lads!"

Neil chipped in "At first I thought you'd signed up to that TV program, you know the one, 'Faking It', where they take a complete no-hoper, give him a job that he's never done, and try and make him successful at it. Doesn't always work out, mind you. You can take a horse to water, and all that." Neil and Wayne found this highly amusing. They loved a bit of craic on the way to work.

Sha took it in his stride. "It's an under-twelve's football team, guys, not England, you know! I won't be getting the sack if results don't come my way, will I?"

"What, you really think it will be easier coaching kids?" said Wayne. "At least the England football team know how to play."

"Not so sure about that," said Neil, "judging by their last result"

Sha didn't even bother to watch England play these days. They always under-performed when it was any major tournament, and it seemed to be all about the individual, and how much money he could get to wear a certain brand of boots. It was everyone out for themselves, rather than for the good of the team and the nation.

Sha saw his role as a coach a little differently. "It's all about teamwork. I'll try to get the boys enjoying playing as a team. The football itself is easy, you just have to run, tackle, kick, and pass the ball or shoot."

Neil and Wayne gave each other a look. They both loved Sha, but he was a bit naive. "Sha, you could be the first managerial casualty of the season, mate," said Wayne. "Look, I know we're taking the Mickey, but seriously, we don't want you getting upset. You take everything to heart. You've got a massive heart, and you wear it on your sleeve. Other people aren't like you. Some of the parents won't be, and Eddie certainly isn't. All we are saying is don't take it to heart if things go wrong."

"Thanks for the lecture. I appreciate what you're saying. Now, can we change the subject?"

Wayne stopped talking and turned the radio up. It was tuned into one of those gold stations, which play hits of the 70s and 80s. The song 'Too Shy' by Kajagoogoo was on. Neil started to sing along, slightly out of tune, but not a bad effort for a Monday morning. "Great song. This is music from my youth. I love this station, it plays all the classics."

It was Sha's turn for a wind-up now. "Does it really? I wasn't listening to this in my youth. You never hear them play 'God save the Queen' or a bit of Discharge!"

Neil had heard this all before, Sha on a rant about music. "It's you Sha, you do it on purpose; you have to be different. All our lives, if it wasn't punk or psychobilly, it was hardcore or grunge. Ska was about the only thing that you liked that was fashionable, and that was only for two years, for normal people."

"I like what I like, I have my own mind."

'Why does he always have to be different?' thought Wayne. "It's called pop music, Sha, because that is what it is, popular music. It sells adverts for the radio station, and people listen to it."

"I can't help it, I'm just being honest. Some of these songs make you want to slit your wrists. I like music to cheer me up, get my feet tapping, put a smile on my face."

Neil had to chip in. "Get your feet tapping and jumping around like a demented Wildebeest, you mean? It's the same with the TV, isn't it Wayne? He can't be like normal people and enjoy a good soap opera."

Neil and Wayne had known each other for such a long time they could work as a tag team winding Sha up. It was almost like they were reading a script. Wayne loved it. "Sha, you say no one watches soap operas, but it's a fact that nineteen million people do."

"Says who?"

"Says the papers. Oh, I forgot. You don't read normal papers either, do you?"

Sha knew they were trying to get a rant out of him, and he was only too willing to oblige. "You guys are like sheep. I listen to punk music because I like it, no other reason. I don't watch the soaps because I don't like them, and I don't read the papers because all they write about is soap stars and their problems. Sometimes they might write about footballers and *their* problems, I'm not really interested in that."

Wayne was getting a bit animated now. "You don't know what you're talking about. I don't watch the soaps all the time, I might catch a bit if the wife has it on.

"About 95% of blokes I know say that," said Sha. He put on a mocking, high-pitched voice. "'It's the wife who watches not me', yet you all know the stories, and talk about nothing else all day. If you are that sad and watch them, just admit it."

Neil didn't agree with that. "Look if I'm sitting down eating my dinner, there isn't much else to do."

This raised a fundamental point for Sha. Most people these days seem to eat dinner off their lap in front of the TV. Sha was old-school. "I like to sit at the dining table with no TV on, and talk to my family. I like to think that's normal. It certainly was in *our* house when I was little."

Neil couldn't comprehend this. "Sha, you're so perfect, aren't you?"

"I'm not perfect, I just like to do what I do. I'm not saying I'm right and you're wrong, we just have to do what we believe is right."

"Couldn't agree more, Sha," said Wayne. "With one exception. The team manager. Welcome to the real world, where things won't always go your way. A world of passion, hatred, joy and pain. And you, my friend, are going to experience most of that. In fact, we reckon you'll last a couple of weeks before you resign."

They pulled up to the house they are working at, and jumped out of the van. Sha loved the fact that his mates believed in him. "Thanks for the vote of confidence chaps, I appreciate it."

Neil busied himself getting the cement mixer sorted, and Sha was sorting his tools out, when Wayne spotted the client coming out of the front door. "Morning love, have you got the kettle on yet?"

She seemed a bit flustered. "Oh, I was just heading off to work. I need to get an early start."

"As soon as you have made the tea, me old darling."

"Oh, ok." She fumbled with her key, trying to get it back in the door.

Wayne gave Neil a little wink. "And while you are in there, three bacon sandwiches wouldn't go amiss. Brown sauce all round, thanks."

Training

Sha and Freddie arrived at training on Wednesday evening. Freddie headed off to meet the boys, and Sha walked up to Eddie. "Evening Eddie."

Eddie didn't turn round from watching the boys warm up. "You turned up, then?"

"I did have some second thoughts."

Eddie stopped him in his tracks. "Oh no you don't! You shot your mouth off about this and that, and now you have to see it through."

A couple of the boys were messing about, so Eddie gave them a bit of abuse, then sent them all off on a lap of the pitch. It was like a four-hundred metre race, with some of the fitter kids running flat out. They all got back to Eddie eventually, and he made the five slowest do press ups. You had to feel sorry for the slower boys; if you sent them round that pitch a hundred times, the same boys would finish last. Some people just aren't built for speed. What better way to treat the slower boys, already knackered from the run, than to make them do press ups in front of the boys that have hardly broken sweat?

Eddie shouted instructions. He was one of those guys who shouts at you rather than talks to you. "A-team with me and Dave, the rest of you with Sha, your new coach." He turned to Sha. "Right you're on your own now Sha, good luck. We'll come back together for a little game at the end of the session." With that, he was off with his team, along with and Dave and a couple of other dads.

Sha was left with his team. "Right boys who usually sorts you out?"

Freddie was the only one to answer. "Someone different every week. Usually one of the dads or mums, depending on who's about."

Sha needed to think on his feet quickly. He hadn't planned the session at all, assuming he'd be able to observe the first week, and take over the next. Then an idea sprang to mind. "Right, we're all going to run around the pitch together. We're not racing, so we only run as fast as the slowest team member." That was a new one on the boys, and they all kind of nodded and set off. They were a bit surprised that Sha set off with them. He set the pace, which was more of a jog than a sprint. Dave and Eddie looked on, wondering what Sha was doing. He was supposed to be training, not jogging around with the boys.

The boys and Sha reached the first corner flag, and he called them to a stop. "Right, we'll do a few press ups together as a team." They all counted them out, and they only got up to five, but that was enough. They jogged to the next corner, then did a few sit ups. Then on to the next, and the last, and they all arrived back together.

"First thing," said Sha, "We work together. Some of you are faster, some of you will be able to tackle better, and get in the way. Some might be brilliant in the air with your head, or be able to take free kicks. We will all be good at something, so let's try and find out what. Get some balls and line up."

The team ran off to get the balls, and Sha called Freddie to him. "I could do with some help, Freddie, I'm not too good with drills and things."

"Great start, Dad," and he gave Sha a cuddle. "I've been reading the FA coaching book. I found it in Eddie's van. He never uses it. I'll set up a ball control drill if you want."

Sha nodded his approval, and Freddie ran after his teammates. It wasn't working out too bad so far, thought Sha, and already he'd shared a nice moment with his son. They soon set up some dribbling and passing exercises. These didn't go that well at first; mostly, the boys were so worried about making a mistake, that they make loads. The strange thing was that Sha didn't shout abuse at them. Instead he was encouraged them, with shouts of "Never mind, try it again. Rome wasn't built in a day, we'll get there." The boys started to feed off this positivity, and they really enjoyed the session.

Eddie wandered over to give his opinion. "I see you're trying to get them to pass the ball? I wouldn't bother, I've tried that, and they're useless."

"They seem to be doing alright. Their confidence seems to be boosted."

"Sometimes Sha, confidence isn't enough. You need to have great ball skills in this game."

"No offence Eddie, but some professional players can't pass a ball. I've heard you shouting that out at the TV screen down the pub. Think of it like music, you don't have to be classically trained to write a pop song, do you? Some of the most popular songs in the world have three chords, written by people who can't read music. If you can play three chords you're in. A bit like football. Keep it simple. The other thing is, we need to mix the teams up a bit. It's not fair your boys giving my boys a beating every week, it can't be good for morale. And you've got eighteen players. I've only got eleven."

Eddie looked thoughtful, which was rare. "Tell you what Sha, you've put yourself out this week, so I *will* mix the teams up a bit, see how we get on. I'll get the boys ready, see what we can do."

As Eddie wandered off, Freddie chatted with his dad. "They usually make us play up the hill as well, to make us look even more stupid."

"It seems to me son, that's the plan. I'm not going anywhere now, till the end of the season. Let's try and enjoy it.'" He ruffled Freddie's hair.

So, all the boys came together for a game, and true to his word, Eddie mixed the teams up. This didn't stop him moaning a lot at the mistakes being made, however, and he changed the teams constantly during the game, subbing this one and that one. Lo and behold, by the end of the game, it was the A-team and all their subs against the B-team, who were playing uphill! Eddie blew the whistle, and called all the boys around. "Two big games this week. A-team, we play Fullershood. It'll be a tough game, 9.30am kick off, same team to start as last week, subs, make sure you all turn up." The subs knew this meant that they wouldn't get a game. They never did. It was great being in the A-team, but it would be nice to actually get a game now and again. "Sha's team, ha ha, I'm calling it Sha's team already, you are playing top of the league Dreton Comets. It'll be tough, seeing as you're at the bottom, but try not to let in any more than ten goals, will you?"

Sha had been wondering why the B-team was in the second division, when surely they would be better off in the third or fourth? Eddie was still chatting to the boys, so Sha asked Dave.

"The thing is, Eddie likes to have teams in the top two divisions. We usually cancel a couple of B-team fixtures during the year, then we can play them at the end of the season, play all the A-team, and avoid relegation with a couple of wins. It makes the club look good."

"Well, that isn't so good for the B-team boys."

"Sha, life is cruel, and there's a learning curve. We're just showing the boys what life's all about. You get nothing in this world for coming second, only abuse. Sha, this team will win nothing, so don't get your hopes up. It'll all end in tears, you know."

The session ended, and Sha and Freddie got in the car and headed towards home. "Thanks Dad, you did really well. I'm proud of you. I heard you sticking up for us."

"Son, I have been too tied up in work, trying to make some money to make us happy, forgetting that we're already happy as a family. Let's see how this pans out. I'm up for it if you are."

They had a little secret handshake, which they did from time to time. Freddie offered up his hand, and his dad duly obliged. Freddie then turned up the CD player, and they both started singing along to a bit of old-school punk.

A Night Out

Sarah was with her Mum. "Thanks for babysitting at such short notice, Mum."

"My pleasure Sarah. I don't see enough of the kids anyway. I never do much these days in the evening anyway."

Sarah and Sha were having a rare night out, the only downside being that Wayne was taking them and going with them, so it was hardly a romantic night for two. A horn beeped outside, announcing Wayne's arrival. He wasn't one for making the effort to get out of the car, but he managed to muster a wave. Sarah gave her mum, Freddie and Louise, her daughter, a kiss. "I'll see you all later. Thanks again Mum. Freddie, go to bed when your Nan tells you, and you too Louise."

"Mum, I'm fifteen!"

Sha entered the room, all smartly dressed. Well, as smart as he ever got, anyway. "We got to go. Come on Sarah, catch you all later."

Sha jumped in the front of the car, and Sarah in the back. Wayne was all excited. "Are you ready for a top night out?"

Hmm, a top night out. Sha's idea of a top night out wasn't down the local pub. He'd rather be heading into London to some dingy dive, to watch an up and coming new band. On the plus side, his mate Sean was playing in a band in the local. On the downside, it was a

Madness tribute band. Wayne couldn't wait. It was one of his favourite bands. "You got your dancing shoes on, Sha? Bit of 'Night Boat To Cairo'!"

Sha quite liked that particular song. "Let's hope they play the first album all the way through, though. It all went a bit downhill after that."

It was the same old argument every time they went to see Sean play. Wayne said "Before you say it Sha, I'm not arguing with you. Madness were better than The Specials. Fact."

Sarah knew that Sha would have to respond, and he did. "The Specials were a ska band. Madness sort of were, then they went a bit pop. You can't argue with that. I liked ska, you liked pop music. I think Sean's band probably play Madness songs better than Madness these days, and they *do* try to ska it up a bit.

Sarah had heard this row a thousand times. "Shut up the pair of you! I've heard this argument so many times! You'll both be dancing all night, and singing your heads off. End of story. Move on."

After this telling off, they both went quiet for a short while. Sha turned the radio on, and tuned it into an indie station. 'Stroke of luck,' thought Sha, as one of his favourite songs, 'Bob' by NOFX blared out. He cranked it up even more, and Sarah joined in with the singing. She'd been a bit brainwashed over the years.

Wayne thought 'Will these two ever grow up?', but kept that thought to himself. His sister however, could read him like a book, and knew exactly what was going through his head.

"We're *not* acting like kids, Wayne, I know what you're thinking. Look at Sha, he's a football manager now, and he's got a big game tomorrow. Are you coming?"

"I might well do, I think Neil wants to come as well. To tell you the truth, I feel a bit sorry for Freddie, I need to give him some support. Sha can just cry on your shoulder, anyway. Here, shouldn't you be at home writing out a strategy for the game?"

"I would be, if you hadn't dragged me out tonight!"

They arrived at the pub, which was quite busy outside. They got inside, and the place was rammed. Music was blaring out from the DJ, and they spotted Sean chatting a couple of young girls up. Sean was forty odd years old, an aging skinhead, still wearing the same clothes he wore when he has sixteen. Mind you, so was half the pub crowd tonight.

They greeted each other, and Sean was pleased Sha could make it. "Thanks mate, I know it's not your cup of tea."

"Seaney, I love all your bands, you know that. I just like to hear *your* songs, better than you playing other people's."

"Yep, and I like to play them, too, but I don't get £150 a night playing my songs, I don't get free beer, and I always get a girl at these gigs."

Sarah gave him a clip round the ear. "About time you settled down and stopped playing the field. Maybe Wayne could get a girl if you stopped shagging them all!" Wayne wasn't impressed, but everyone else had a laugh.

This being the local, with a band that suited people of a certain age, just about the whole village was out, plus people from the neighbouring villages. Inevitably, Eddie and Dave were in the pub. You could say what you liked about Eddie and Dave, they had some pretty bad ideas about the way the world worked, but when it came to buying drinks, they were straight to the bar. They walked over to the others with a tray of drinks.

"Sha, get your mouth round this lot. You're going to need it for tomorrow." Yep, Sha was copping it as always. Eddie and Dave had the old-style clobber on, as well as Sean. Dave's top looked like it was from 1979, frayed at the edges, and a bit stretched, to say the least. There was a four-inch gap from Dave's trousers to the underside of his Fred Perry. Years of drinking had gone into that expansion of the midriff.

"Nice clobber boys," Sean was eager to point out.

"This was the fashion back in 1979," said Eddie.

"You're all living in a time warp," pointed out Sha.

Dave was about to say something to Sha when a nudge from behind caused him to spill half his pint. "Oi, what's your bleedin' game?"

The man didn't seem phased. "Alright mate, put your dummy back in." A bit of high testosterone followed, with Dave and Eddie having a stare-off against three other forty-year olds dressed all the same.

Sarah has seen it all before many times, and she was glad Sha wasn't getting involved. "Don't these people realise how stupid they are, Sha? They're all acting like they did twenty odd years ago."

Sha was gloating. "You're *so* lucky you married me!" She *did* love him. He still had that cheeky grin he had when they were young.

The band was about to start, and the audience was alive with anticipation. The singer came out and gave it the 'Alright?' chat, geeing the audience up. When he intoned the words, 'One Step Beyond,' the place went mental. If you've never been to a ska gig, it's hard to explain the energy. Once you love ska it never leaves you. You might drift off into other forms of music from time to time, but as soon as you hear it again, your feet can't stay still.

Sha wasn't on the dance floor, and Sarah was puzzled! "Sha, you not dancing?"

"Sarah, I need a few more drinks. This lot never get out much, and they'll be all worn out in a minute. And you just know there's gonna be a scuffle any minute. Why do people try and stand at the front of a gig with a drink, and not just get out there to dance? It's a bloody mystery to me, someone's girlfriend will have a drink knocked out of her hand, then it'll be handbags at ten paces." Sure enough, just as Sha said it, something was kicking off. It all quietened down, but Sha wasn't in the mood for a dance just yet. "When we go to London, The Astoria, Brixton or Camden, you never see any trouble. But here you get this small town mentality. My village is bigger than yours."

They decided to hit the bar, and ended up staying there for about an hour. The drink was flowing now, and the mood in the whole place had mellowed a bit. Wayne came bounding over. "This is bloody brilliant! Best night ever!"

"You need to get out more in London Wayne," said Sha. "Next time we go, we'll take you with us."

"I was reading about nights out in London in the paper." Sarah pushed Wayne back on the dance floor. She'd had enough of bickering for one night. She grabbed Sha, and pulled him onto the dance floor too, and that's where they stayed till the end of the gig.

They ended up getting a taxi home. Wayne decided to walk it off a bit with Eddie and Dave. They arrived home, and both of them were having trouble trying to get the key in the door. Sha was singing one of the tunes from earlier.

Sarah's mum heard all the commotion, and opened the door. She gave them a bit of a stern look. "I can see *you* had a good night then?"

"Hello to the sexiest mother-in-law in the world."

Sarah's mum grabbed her coat; it was time for her to get off home. Sarah was grateful to her mum, and said "Thanks Mum. Kids OK?"

"Yes, fine love. I'll let you get Sha in. He seems to be struggling to get in the door. I'll give you a call you tomorrow."

They managed to get upstairs without waking the kids. Sha went into the bathroom first. Sarah started getting undressed. She had treated herself to some new underwear, and was feeling quite sexy. Sha came out of the bathroom, saw her, and got a wee bit excited. He fell over trying to get his trousers off. She helped him with this, then went into the bathroom.

She was in the mood for a bit of love-making herself tonight. It had been a nice night off from mothering and wifely duties. She slipped into bed beside him, and kissed him. He was fast asleep. Or maybe unconscious. One of the two, anyway. She gave him another kiss on the forehead, and whispered in his ear. "I love you. See you in the morning."

First Game

And so the big day came, the first game with Sha in charge. They arrived at the playing fields full of hope and trepidation. They walked towards the pitch. The A-team game had already kicked off. It came as no surprise to Sha and Freddie that the first thing they heard as they approached the pitch was Eddie's voice, shouting. Also evident were Dave's dulcet tones, pretty much on the off-beat to Eddie's bellowing. What with the odd mum and dad chipping in, there was a chorus of abuse.

Sha gathered his team together for a chat. "First thing first, I'm *not* going to say it's not about the winning, it's the taking part, because we all *know* we want to win if we can. What I want to say is it *is* about playing to the best of your ability, and enjoying the game. Football seems to have lost its way in recent years, with the money, irresponsible role models, and all the aggression, but I want *you* to be respectful. Don't argue with the referee. Call him 'Sir', like in rugby, and walk away from trouble. We might win the fair play award at the end of the season."

Robbo sniggered. "I'd rather win the league!"

"So would I Robbo, but I'm afraid that won't happen this year. Come on, cheer up. If we don't win the fair play award, we might win the cup!" The boys were quite chuffed with Sha's enthusiasm, but they had got used to going out of the cup in the first round. "I forgot to tell you guys, Eddie told me last night that we got a bye in the first round. That means we are into the second round already. First win chalked up already, hey guys?" The boys let out a cheer and ran off together to warm up as a team.

The ref blew the whistle, and the A-team game finished. Seven-nil win. 'Not bad,' you might think, but Eddie was still moaning as his players gathered round. "That should have been ten-nil at least. What were you doing out there?"

One of the boys couldn't believe what he was hearing. "What do we have to do to please you, Eddie?"

"What do you have to do to please me? I'll tell you. You demolish the opposition. *That's* what you have to do, demolish them. I want to win the league *and* the cup *and* do it in style. Let everyone know we are unbeatable." Some of the over-exuberant dads joined in with a bit of cheering. They loved the fact that their boys were part of such a winning side. Some of them were under the illusion that their boys would go on to play Premiership football and earn millions. Perhaps some of them needed to wake up and smell the coffee. They conveniently avoided the fact that only a very few boys go on to such success, and it was a safe bet that it wouldn't be three quarters of this team!

Eddie dismissed his team. No doubt he would continue with his rant at training during the week. One of his players came up, a tiny little fellow called Dylan, who normally didn't say much at all. His mother was an African lady, who had been at the game to watch her son. She didn't always make it to the games, and neither did her husband, as they both worked unsociable hours, trying to make ends meet. She kept herself to herself. Or was it that no one ever really talked to her, apart from a quick 'hello'? The mums and dads watching the A-team were something of a clique, who had all known each other for years, and just tended to talk to each other. There wasn't any malice in them, it was just that they had their circle of friends, and were quite happy with that. Dylan's mum had told him to speak to the coach if he was unhappy about something, and hence he was standing in front of Eddie.

He raised the courage to speak. "Eddie?"

"What do you want, Dylan?"

"It's just that I've been sub for nine weeks now, and never had a game."

"I've told you before Dylan, I can't change a winning team. You'll get your chance sooner or later."

"But we were four-nil up by half-time."

Eddie's patience was running out. "What are you saying, Dylan?"

"I'd like to play for the B-team. They don't have any subs, so I might get a bit of a game."

Eddie just couldn't understand some kids. "You're too good for that team. You're part of the A-team squad."

"So you say, but I don't seem to be good enough for your team."

Sha was standing nearby, and overheard the conversation.

"Hey Eddie, he can come and play for us if he wants. We'd be very grateful to have a sub."

Eddie did not like to be questioned, and his gnarly, angry face appeared. "You want him, you have him. He doesn't want to be in my squad, he's all yours." He then stormed off, muttering under his breath.

Sha turned to Dylan, who looked a bit worried after Eddie's outburst. Sha put his arm around him. "Dylan, you can be a sub to start, but I promise I will get you on the pitch second half."

Dylan's face lit up, and he walked over to the rest of the team with Sha. "Guys, meet our new team member, Dylan." The boys gathered round, shook Dylan's hand and patted him on the back. He was one of those boys that everyone took to.

Dylan's mother came up and shook Sha's hand. "Thank you. He just wants to play football. It is all he ever talks about. Every Sunday morning, I go into his room and he has his kit all laid out ready on his bed. He gets so excited! Then every Sunday afternoon he just goes quiet. We tell him next week he will get his chance, but he never does."

Sha, being the big softy that he was, felt a lump in his throat. Now he had the task of having to sub one of the other players off during the game, to give Dylan a chance. It was his first game in charge, and he didn't want to upset anybody. He told Dylan's mum he would get Dylan on during the early part of the second half. He secretly thought that he might have to take his own son off, to avoid upsetting anyone else. Oh, the joys of being a football coach!

The game kicked off, and things went well for the first ten minutes. Then the inevitable happened, and it was one-nil to the opposition. Soon it was two-nil, and then three-nil. They consolidated a bit, but the opposing team were very strong, and got a fourth just before half-time.

Sha beckoned the lads over. "Never mind lads, keep your chins up. This team are the strongest in the league, and had a sixteen-nil win last week. I think you're doing great. We are a team, and we need to work together more. Encourage your teammates. Help them out. Try to play the ball a bit wider. They're pushing up loads on the flanks, and they all want to score. Let's try and get our wingers in the game. Look, let's pretend its nil-nil, and see how we get on second half. Five more minutes, then I'm going to rotate the team. Don't worry if you get subbed off, I just want to give everyone a chance. And hey, enjoy yourselves out there! That's what we're here for!"

Sha felt quite pleased with his first half-time team talk, and the boys couldn't believe they weren't getting shouted at. They headed back to the pitch with renewed confidence, and Robbo turned to Freddie. "He's alright, your dad."

Freddie smiled back, and thought 'Yes, he *is* alright.' He felt a sudden swell of pride and confidence.

The second half started better. The other team went all-out in attack, thinking they could score twenty. The boys had listened to Sha and tried to move the ball wide. It wasn't always working, but they started to improve. Martin, the keeper, made a great save and fed the ball out quickly to the right wing. A quick pass forward from the full-back put James through on the wing. He ran with the ball as if his life depended on it, cutting inside to head for goal. A crashing two-footed tackle took him down, and the ref blew the whistle. James's dad went running on to see if he was OK. He wasn't. His ankle had swollen up already.

Sha turned to Dylan. "You're on son, go and enjoy it."

Dylan couldn't believe it! He was going to play! He ran straight over to where the free kick was going to be taken. Freddie was ready to take the free kick, and the defenders had come upfield to hopefully head it into the net for a goal. The kick was about six yards outside the box, slightly over to the right. Dylan was standing beside Freddie, and he whispered in Freddie's ear. "Can I take it Freddie? I can score from here."

It was a long way out, but Freddie knew that Dylan had one hell of a powerful kick. But from here? He decided to let him have a go. "I'll fake it, and you give it a go, Dylan."

Dylan nodded in agreement, and fixed his eye on the ball, and then the goal and goalkeeper. The ref blew the whistle. Freddie ran up and over the ball, causing a bit of confusion in the box as players jockeyed for position. Dylan ran up and gave the ball an almighty thump. It rose over the wall, and dipped like you wouldn't believe! The goalkeeper was rooted to the spot, and didn't have time to move, as the ball crashed into the back of the net.

For one split second, the team were stunned. Then they went crazy! Sha was jumping about on the sideline. He couldn't believe it! What a foot that Dylan's got! The manager of the other team was also stunned. In all his time coaching kids' football, he'd never seen a kick like that.

The game restarted, and was a much more evenly-played affair. It's funny what a difference a bit of confidence can make. The final whistle blew, and you would be forgiven for thinking that Little Olney had won the game. The boys finally gathered round Sha for a debrief. "What can I say? Brilliant, every one of you. OK, maybe we lost 4-1, but we won the second half. Did you hear that? We won the second half, against the best side in the league. Enjoy that feeling, and see you all at training next week."

A simple thing like scoring a goal can make a massive difference to morale. Over the next few weeks, the team just got better and better. Sha had a big smile on his face all the time, and Wayne and Neil could notice the difference in him when he gave them a hand at work.

They still liked to give him a bit of banter though, especially Wayne. "How have results been going Sven?"

"Four games, no wins, but we are all trying, and getting closer to that victory."

"Fair play to you Sha, them kids are brimming with confidence, I hear."

"We just need a win!"

"Who have you got this week?"

"Dulwood, in the cup."

"Oh well Sha, better luck next week."

The Cup

It was a beautiful day for a cup game. The sun was out, and there was a great sense of excitement and anticipation in the air. The team were ready to start, and more and more parents were turning up to watch their children play. Sarah was at the game too, along with her daughter Louise, and her friend. The only thing that wasn't perfect was that the opposition hadn't turned up yet.

The referee was getting a bit impatient. He wasn't happy that they were an hour late. "If Dulwood don't turn up shortly, they'll have to forfeit the game."

"I'm sure they'll make it, ref," said Sha.

Sarah turned to Sha. "Hey, you could be on for another win here!"

Freddie and the boys were getting restless. There are only so many times you can run through your drills. Louise and her friend decided to go and watch the under sixteens, who were playing on another pitch.

Finally, the ref's patience ran out. He had another game to officiate after this one, and he was already running late. He blew his whistle. "That's it. Game awarded to Little Olney." The ref shook Sha's hand, and started to walk off. Sha's team and their parents realised that they had reached the third round of the cup, and started to cheer. It didn't matter to them they hadn't had to play yet. Getting knocked out in the third round sounds a lot better than getting knocked out in the first or second round.

A rather rotund, red-faced man came bounding over, kind of half-running, half-skipping. "Where's the ref? We're Dulwood. Sorry we're a tad late. Bit of a late night. Damn these 10am kick offs on a Sunday!"

The ref was not impressed, and he walked back over. "You are over an hour late. You have forfeited the game. It will all be in my report."

The large coach wasn't very happy. He had been joined by a few of his players' parents, one of whom was in no mood to take this lying down. "Ref, just play the fucking game. What difference does it make?"

The ref was quite a mellow chap. He was a schoolteacher by day, and had come across this sort of parent many a time. The swearing didn't impress him. "Now, let's keep a lid on the swearing please. I have another game to referee, and I'm late already. Any complaints, write to the league."

This didn't go down very well. "You can't talk to us like that, mate. We are Dulwood. Nobody talks to us like that."

Sha had a quiet word with the ref. "I think you need to make a swift exit. It could get nasty." The ref nodded in agreement, and headed off. Sha then tried to defuse the situation. "Guys, it is not the ref's fault. He has to go."

The big fellow let rip at the ref as he trotted off. "You are out of fucking order, ref! Well out of order!" Then he looked at Sha. "And you … your crappy B-team couldn't beat our C-team, let alone us."

One of the other dads shouted after the ref. "Wanker!" A few more joined in for good measure, raising their hands in the traditional gesture. Sha decided it was time to get his lot moving as well, before it all kicked off.

'What an absolute joy coaching would be on a Sunday morning if all the adults stayed at home!', Sha thought to himself later. 'People need to lighten up a bit.'

Wayne

Another week, another training session! Sha's team, on the back of the cup walkover, had managed to draw their last two games. The training ground had become a place of enjoyment. Today when Sha turned up his team were already running round the pitch together, laughing and joking as they went round.

Eddie was his usual miserable self. "Sha, you've had a couple of draws and a bye, and a walkover in the cup. You'd never have beaten Dulwood."

"I know that, but we got through. Changing goalkeepers and moving Martin into defence has made a big difference. Two clean sheets. We're getting like Liverpool when Alan Hansen played. No one was going to score. I'm going to change the midfield this week, see what happens. I need a playmaker."

"Bloody hell, you're getting a bit cocky! Another three months and you'll be managing Arsenal!"

"Just doing my best Eddie." He ran off and joined his team.

Wayne had turned up, in his jogging pants and boots. He had been threatening to come down to training for a while. Wayne had been a fantastic sportsman when he was younger. He could outrun people, had terrific ball skills in rugby and football, and was a pretty good bowler at cricket. When he was fifteen, his world had come tumbling down. He got knocked off his pushbike, and his knee had never been the same since. He left school and started working, and had never been involved with sport again, only watching from the armchair.

So here he was, ready to get involved. This was a massive boost for Sha. Wayne would know where to play everyone, just by watching for ten minutes. He joked with Sha. "I can't handle you not winning a game this year. I owe it to you and my nephew to help sort this out. Who have you got next up?"

"Hitchdon in the cup."

"Well that is the easiest game you could get. You never know, we might get the win!"

It was a great training session. Wayne knew a few different drills, and it's always good to keep things fresh at training. If you looked over at Eddie and Dave's training, it was more about Eddie liking the sound of his own voice, and re-living his first team appearance for the local town. Their drills didn't involve all the team members, and some would just stand around for ages, while Eddie's favourites got special attention.

The session neared its end, and Eddie brought his team over for the usual game in which his boys could give the B-team a good thrashing. Wayne wasn't having any of that. He wanted to carry on with what he was doing. Eddie was surprised at Wayne, wasting his time with this lot. He knew how good Wayne had once been, and he also knew not to argue with Wayne if he said 'no.' Eddie and his boys trudged off.

Sha looked at Wayne for an explanation. "Look Sha, you build confidence through a session, you don't want that knocked straight back out of them." It was a fair point. "Now, I know you have been rotating the captain's armband to give everyone a go, that's very noble, and speaking to the boys, those who wanted a go have all had a go. It's your team, but I have a couple of ideas. Can I?"

Sha had so much respect for Wayne, and knew that whatever he suggested would work. He had a good eye. He called the team over to listen to Wayne. "First up, that was fantastic guys, well done. We're going to have a little game, you against us dads that are here, and mums too, if you want to get involved. No tackling in the game, we can't afford any injuries, and I have to go to work tomorrow. The idea is passing the ball. Three touches maximum, or you lose possession. We want *you* to have the ball. Us dads will just try and cut the pass out. Freddie, I want you just in front of the defence, Robbo go up front. Dylan, I want you in midfield as well, drifting anywhere you want, apart from defence. Come on, let's go!"

They played for half an hour, while Eddie and his team finished off and headed home. Sometimes you look at this type of session and you wonder who is enjoying it more the, dads or the lads. Everyone enjoyed this one though, and it proved both useful and fun.

The game concluded, and Wayne had a chat with Sha before announcing the team for the big cup game. "Freddie will be just in front of the defence as the playmaker. Let's try and play through him. He will also be captain." All the boys and parents agreed. He ran through the rest of the team, which was pretty much the same apart from Dylan getting a free role to roam all over the place. Sha thanked Wayne, and everyone headed home, full of anticipation for the weekend game coming up.

Freddie and Sha were in the car heading home, and Freddie turned to his dad. "Thanks Dad, for what you're doing. And it was great to get uncle Wayne involved! I can't believe I'm captain!"

"The thing is son, I always thought you should be captain. You talk to every player constantly through the game. I couldn't make my own son captain myself, it wouldn't seem right. Wayne knows what he is talking about, and I think you'll play well where he said. I'm just annoyed I never thought of it! I love being the coach, but technically I'm not good enough. It's alright for this year, but as you get older you'll need a better coach. I'm hoping Wayne'll take up the mantle. The trouble with me son, is I like to try different things. Some dads start coaching their sons at six, and go right through until they are seventeen, which is fantastic. That's a big commitment, which is something I'm not very good at. Look at me. I've played sport, played in bands, had my own business, and now I'm writing books. I tend to get bored with things very quickly. The only thing I like to keep the same is my family."

"It's like you always say, Dad, it's a big wide world out there."

"Yep, and your sister hit the nail on the head last week when she said 'You're not here for a long time, you're here for a good time.' I loved that expression because she's so right. Work is fantastic, don't get me wrong, I've always loved it, but it's the other things as well that count. Now I know I have been chasing my tail the last couple of years, but I'm now back in the zone. I've never told you this son, but I got picked on at school for being a bit different in the way I looked. I had to live with it, and twenty-five years down the line, I still see those people. Some of them ended up in prison, some ended up divorced, but most of them ended up going to the same pub they've been going to since we were young."

"I see what you're saying Dad. I'm going to enjoy my life and be like you and Mum. First things first though, let's win the game Sunday." They gave the secret handshake, and whacked up the CD player.

Game on

Another round of cup games, and both teams were at home again. Luckily they hadn't been drawn against each other, which might have spoiled Sha's season. The games were about to kick off, being played at the same time, on pitches next to each other.

Eddie was doing his team talk by one pitch, and Sha by the other.

Eddie: "Anyone makes a mistake, you'll be off the pitch as quick as you like. We've got plenty on the bench."

Sha: "If anyone makes a mistake, don't worry about it. We'll all get behind you. I don't want to hear any moaning."

Eddie: "Let people know if they are cocking it up. We need to win by at least six goals."

Sha: "It only takes one goal to win it."

Eddie: "Tackle hard, and get in the ref's face."

Sha: "Be careful in the tackle, and remember, what the ref says goes."

The games kicked off, and the running commentaries continued from both camps.

Eddie: "Jesus! How did you miss that tackle! That was SHIT!"

Sha: "Unlucky, you can catch him next time."

Eddie: "Offside ref!"

Sha: "That was close guys, keep trying."

The two coaching styles were very different. Who could say what was right and wrong? Half-time arrived and was nil-nil in both games. The half-time team talks were also very different.

Eddie: "What's the matter with you lot? That's shit, the worst half all season."

Sha: "Guys, I can't praise you enough, what a team effort!"

Eddie: "Clive you're off. You've been running around like a headless fucking chicken. Hilly, get them working out there this is shocking."

Sha: "I'm going to throw Martin into the attack. Craig, you drop to defence. We need a tall guy up front."

The second halves started, and Wayne questioned Sha's thinking about Martin.

Sha explained. "I just feel if he's in the box, they'll try to mark him, and we might sneak a player in unmarked to score. The other team's gonna be thinking he's gonna head the ball. They don't know he's not great in the air."

Both games continued. Eddie's side got a few lucky breaks, which seemed to unsettle their opponents, and they quickly took advantage, going two up. Sha's team were having no luck at all. They hadn't had many chances, in what was a fast game. With only a couple of minutes to go, they got a free kick. It was out of Dylan's range, but he stepped up to take it anyway. People were shouting at him to play it in to feet, but he knew exactly where he was going to place it. There was a lot of running around before he took it, but he concentrated only on Martin's head, not moving at all, and about half a foot taller than everyone else.

He absolutely drove the ball towards that big head. The ball seemed to be going one way, and everyone followed its flight, except Martin. Suddenly, the path of the ball began to bend. Before Martin knew anything about it, the ball hit the side of his head, knocking him straight over, and ricocheting into the net! This might be their first win! They just had to keep calm. Martin was a bit dazed, and had to come off, leaving them a man down. Resolute, they managed to hold on, and record their first win of the season. What a feeling! Long overdue.

Eddie's game had finished a couple of minutes earlier, and he had seen the goal. "Well done Sha, lucky win, but a win is a win. Let's hope you don't meet *us* in the quarter finals."

'He couldn't just say 'well done'', thought Wayne. As Eddie strolled off, Wayne gave him the finger.

Sha pulled Wayne's hand down. "No Wayne we are better than that."

Sha then gave Eddie the finger with both hands, and he and Wayne burst out laughing.

School

Hilly, Eddie's son, was walking down the corridor. He was nicknamed 'Hilly' because of his temperament, up one minute, and down the next. A bit like his father, he thought he knew everything, and wasn't afraid to tell you so. He was hanging with his mates Stevo and Paul, who played in the A-team with him.

Dylan and Freddie were coming along in the opposite direction. Hilly was first to open his mouth. "You were so lucky to get that win! Don't be getting ideas about winning that cup. It's got our name written all over it."

Stevo piped up in support. "Yeah, you boys are getting a bit big for your boots."

"You sound like you're getting a bit worried," said Dylan.

Hilly always had an answer. "You should be in *our* team Dylan, not that crappy B-team. Oh, wait a minute, you *were* in our team, and couldn't get a game. Perhaps you *are* in the right team."

Dylan, ever the optimist, said "I thought we *were* the same team. We all play for Little Olney, don't we?"

Hilly and his pals all laughed, and Hilly replied "My dad said he doesn't even *need* you losers at the club. Same team, my arse!"

Freddie was getting a bit upset at this, as he didn't like people bad-mouthing his dad. Dylan could see what was going on. "I love playing in Sha's team. We all get a chance to play, and everybody is happy, whether we win, lose or draw. You'd better remember, if we *do* get to play you in the cup, we have nothing to lose. You, on the other hand ..."

A couple of girls had been standing nearby, Jessica and her friend Wendy. Wendy was never short of a few words, and she wanted to offer Hilly a few now. "Shut up Hilly. Or is it Pricky? You can kick a ball about, so what! Your personality is about as electric as a flat battery."

Jessica was keen to add more. "Look mate, this time next year everyone might be better at football than you, and your face won't get any better. You're not as hard as you like to think. Now take your two halfwits and piss off, unless you want me to get my brother."

They made a swift exit. You didn't want to mess with Jessica's brother. He was a quiet bloke, who used to get pushed around a lot until he cracked one day, and took out the three hardest blokes in the school in one short outburst. No, best to head off. They could deal with these two another time.

Jessica asked Freddie how he was. "I'm good thanks Jessica, you certainly told them."

"Well, he thinks he's gonna be the next David Beckham. So do ten million other boys. Probably end up in the pub every night for the next twenty-five years, talking about what might have been. Can me and Wendy come and watch you Sunday?"

"Yeah sure, no worries, see you then." They walked off in different directions.

Freddie turned to Dylan. "Strange that, why would she want to come and watch me play football? I don't think she even likes football."

"She wants to see you Freddie. Are you blind? She's got the hots for you, man!"

"Oh, didn't notice. Maybe Wendy has the hots for you, Dylan."

"I sure hope so."

Quarter Final

The team talk was done. Every boy knew what he had to do. This might be a game too far for the boys, but they had come a long way. Could they possibly? Sarah gave her son a kiss on the head. Sha started singing 'He's a lover man, Freddie.' He'd mentioned the conversation with Jessica to his mum, and she'd obviously told Sha about it. Freddie just shook his head and walked out onto the pitch.

Sha shouted after him "Need any advice son, I wrote the *book* on love!"

OMG! Why did dads have to act so stupid? He gave his dad one of those 'stop embarrassing me' looks.

It was a big family day out. Louise his sister, and her friend were down to watch. They decided they didn't want to be hanging around parents, and walked over to the other side of the pitch. Wayne and Sha looked worried. It had been an incredible achievement to get this far, and neither of them wanted the cup run to end. The boys came under a lot of pressure in the first half, but they soaked it up well, and were glad when half-time arrived.

Sha was his usual optimistic self. "Great work lads! This team were third in division one last year. We can beat them!"

"They're all over us, Dad!"

"True, yes, but we need to get hold of the ball, move it quickly like we always do. They're tiring already. Come on, get back out there and enjoy it."

The game kicked off again, with Little Olney starting to get more of the ball, as the other team indeed began to tire, making a couple of substitutions, bringing on fresh legs. It made no difference, and Little Olney grew in confidence, seemingly brimming with stamina.

The other team had one more sub to bring on. A lad who had just turned up, hastily put a kit on. He was a big, physical lad, and made an immediate impact out on the pitch, elbowing the keeper during a corner, and heading a goal. For once, Little Olney protested but to no avail. The ref hadn't seen the foul, and the goal stood. The new player ran rings around the team for the next ten minutes, and added a second goal right at the end.

The dream was shattered, the coaches were shattered and so were the boys. They all gathered round at the end. Sha said to them "Guys, you played fantastic. If it wasn't for that big lad, you had the game won. He was too physical for you. We need to work on that next week at training."

Nobody else said anything at all. Sha looked over to the other side of the pitch, where he could see his daughter Louise and her friend talking to the ref. Also, the other team seemed to be getting irate about something. Sha ran over to see what was going on.

"Dad, they cheated. We heard them say that boy was fourteen, and we think we know who he is."

The ref approached, and apologised to Sha. "I should have realised, the size of that boy. They will be fined, and have to forfeit the game."

Sha picked Louise and her mate up, one in each arm (they were actually a bit big for this), and spun them round. "Well done girls, well spotted."

News quickly spread, and there were some joyous scenes! Sha awarded Louise and her friend the 'man of the match' award, and the boys carried them off the pitch.

Wayne couldn't believe it either. "You couldn't write the script! Semi-final here we come!"

Back At The House

Wayne, Sha and Neil were sitting around the breakfast table, and Sarah was busying herself at the sink. They were all re-living the joys of the quarter-final performance. There *was* one downside to the victory, though. The draw had been made for the semi-finals, and they had been drawn against Eddie's team.

"It was bound to happen sooner or later," said Wayne. "I'm beginning to think it might have been better if we'd lost the last game. Can you imagine losing to Eddie? Oh my god, that will be the biggest thing that ever happens in his life."

Neil was showing some support. "Come on the Bs."

Sha was feeling serious, though, contemplating their route to the semi, and didn't feel like joining in with Neil. "A bye in the first round, the second-round team didn't show, we won the third, and the fourth the other team got disqualified! Now we have to play Eddie's team, who are top of the division and haven't lost a game all year. It's like a flipping screenplay or something!"

Wayne was in a philosophical mood. "Sometimes your name is just on the cup. We've had such good luck, and we're unbeaten for five games in the league. I know it's a division below, but we're doing alright. They've got everything to lose. We've got nothing to lose, and we've come so far."

Sarah, who had been listening in, shook her head. "It's just a game, guys. Remember that." She shouted up to Freddie. "Are you ready for school yet?" He and Louise came bundling down the stairs.

Wayne sometimes liked to play the annoying uncle, and offered Louise a lift, knowing full well what the reply was going to be.

"In that heap? With you lot? You've got to be joking! I'll walk, but thanks for the offer."

Wayne grabbed her and started to tickle her, in that annoying way uncles do. "Too old to give your uncle a cuddle?"

She did her best not to laugh, but it was a bit much for her. "Get off me, get a life uncle!"

Neil started to move his head from side to side, wagging his finger, and saying "Don't even go there girlfriend!"

Wayne and Neil got the "Whatever" from Louise, and she was out the door.

The men and Freddie said their goodbyes to Sarah, and jumped in the van. Freddie was in the back of course; he was still only the boy. As usual, Wayne had some load of crap on the radio, so Sha pulled out a CD and shoved it on. The sound of The Beat singing 'Best Friend' came blaring out. Freddie knew that this would be an embarrassing trip for him. It was 8am, and these three so-called adults were singing, hitting the steering wheel and zigzagging down the road. They pulled up at a red light, all grinning, and Neil shouted out "Red Light!" They all jumped out, and started dancing round the van. Wayne jumped up on the roof. The lights changed, and they all jumped back in. The cars behind were beeping, and someone pulled up beside them and told them to grow up. He duly got told where to go.

They pulled up at Freddie's school, and he jumped out. "I'll walk home, thanks." He turned, and bumped into Jessica. Luckily for him, the van pulled away.

"Hi Freddie."

"Oh, hi Jessica, sorry about falling into you like that."

"No worries. I enjoyed the game, by the way. Sorry we arrived a bit late, and by the time we were going to say hello, you all got a bit excited, and then you were gone."

"Sorry Jessica I would like to have seen you."

"You would? I didn't think you were that bothered."

"Yes I am." He blushed. "I mean, no, I'm not. I mean yes, erm … do you want to go to the cinema sometime? You don't have to, only if you want to, I mean."

She had to jump in, as he was getting a bit flustered. "That would be great. We can talk about it later."

Off she went. Freddie was well chuffed. Today wasn't too bad after all, and he had a grin like a cat that had just got the cream.

"What are you smiling at?" It was Hilly and his sidekicks.

"Yeah, what are you smiling at?", sneered Stevo.

"What is there an echo in here?" said Hilly. Hilly liked to be the big man, especially when his mates were with him. "My dad is getting a bit fed up with your dad thinking he can manage a team of weirdos. He says you are well-suited, as your dad was always a weirdo with no mates."

This was like a red rag to a bull. Freddie could take abuse about himself, but not about his family.

He grabbed Hilly by the throat. "Say that again about my dad, and I'll knock you out." Before he could do anything, the other two had grabbed him and pushed him up against the wall. This could go terribly wrong for Freddie.

It is always handy to have a big sister at school, and luckily for Freddie, his was just coming by. She pushed Stevo to the floor, and dragged the other two off, with the help of two of her male classmates. "Do we have a problem here Freddie?"

"No problem, sis."

The three boys saw who was with Louise, and ran off quickly. "Freddie, I'm here if you need me."

One of the boys with her asked "Hey, do you know my little sister Jessica? How funny, Louise! Jessica's got the hots for your little brother!"

Freddie blushed. Louise noticed straight away, as a big sister would. "Looks like it's a mutual admiration, hey Freddie?"

Freddie was beginning to wish his big sister hadn't come by.

The Evening Before

It was the evening before the big semi-final day. Sarah and Sha were in the living room, while Freddie and Louise were in their bedrooms. Sarah was troubled over Freddie. "You'll have to go and talk to him Sha. He's worried to death."

"He isn't the only one Sarah. I can't believe we'e got to this situation. I signed up to help them out, maybe win one game, that was the objective."

She couldn't help but smile. Her two men were both so soft. Louise was more like her, and just got on with things, but these two took everything to heart. "You should be very proud of yourself Sha, you're hardly typical coaching material. The boys love you, that's all that matters. You can hold your head high, no matter what happens. But if you can beat that twat Eddie all the better."

"Sarah, that's unlike you! You're right though, he *is* a twat. And while we are on the subject, he's also a miserable, selfish bastard. Some of them kids have hardly played any football all year." Sha needed to get that off his chest. Sometimes you just need to let things out.

He headed upstairs to see Freddie. He entered the room. "You OK son?"

Freddie looked up. He was just lying on his bed, listening to some music. He nodded.

'That's a good song you're listening to."

'Sometimes you just need a bit of music in your life, Dad." His son was very like him. They both had a love of music and life. "Dad, I'm not that bothered about winning the cup, you know that, it's just the abuse for the next five years that bothers me."

Louise was just walking past the door. "You won't get any abuse Freddie, not with me about."

She was such a good sister. Sha cuddled them both. "Me and your mum are so proud of you both. It's a game of football, that's it. If we lose, so what? But let's enjoy the day. Now crank that music up and sing yourself to sleep."

The Big Day

Usually a semi-final might attract forty to fifty parents. Today, half the village was out, literally hundreds of people. Dylan looked out of the changing room window. "Oh my god, have you lot seen the crowd?" They all scampered over for a look. There was a sea of people, from old to young, and including most of the school.

Wayne and Sha walked in, and the last few boys. Ryan and Jordan were listening to Sha's iPod, jumping about all over the place. These two were usually the quiet ones.

"Dad, what the hell are they listening to."

Sha went over to check it out, and the lyrics were screaming out 'Who the fuck are you, telling me what to do, said who the fuck are you?"

"Blimey Dad, that's a bit near the mark!"

"Oh it's a song called 'Blunt' by a band called Tetsu. Check it out on YouTube. It could have been written about Eddie. It seems to be getting the boys in the mood for the game."

Sha didn't like to swear in front of the boys, but he thought the track might have the desired effect, without him having to do any swearing. Every team had a song, apparently.

In his dressing room, Eddie didn't need a music track. He always sang to his own tune. "No less than twenty-nil today, and I mean it. Tackle harder than ever. I don't mind if they get hurt."

Joey, the quietest lad in Eddie's team, spoke up. "Do we *really* want to hurt people? My best mate plays in the other team." He was referring to Robbo. They had been mates for years.

"Are you questioning me, boy?" Silence. "What, cat got your tongue now?" Still no answer. "Right you're sub. Jimmy, swap shirts."

With that, Joey jumped up, threw off his shirt, and shouted "To be honest, I've had enough of this! My dad said I'd be better off in church on Sunday mornings. And do you know what? I think he was right." He stormed out of the changing room.

Eddie was seething. The big day hadn't started well. Dave had to jump in to calm everybody down.

Joey walked past the other dressing room, looking down, his arms held stiffly by his sides, and with his fists and teeth clenched. Robbo saw him, and ran out.

"Hey, what's up Joey?"

"Nothing. I'm off to church with my dad. Good luck. I'll see you later."

Robbo headed back in. All the boys were dancing to ska music, following Sha and Wayne around the room. This beats running round the pitch, that's for sure! Eddie's team walked past on their way to the pitch, catching glimpses of them dancing. They were the ones looking tense, not Sha's boys.

The time had come to get out to the pitch. Wayne decided to have a last word with the team. "Right boys, if we lose, we lose. It's no skin off our noses, right? Enjoy it, do your best, and if we can pull it off, let's win it for Sha. What do you say?"

They all shouted "Yeah!" and went charging out onto the pitch.

Game time is here. The teams are ready, and the crowd is very boisterous. The ref counts the players, checks the linesman, and blows for kick off. The B-team kick off. Freddie passes it to Dylan.

Wayne turns to Sha. "If we can hold them until half-time, we may have a chance. Come on Dylan!"

Dylan looks up, and sees Hilly arguing with his own goalkeeper. The goalkeeper is well off his line. Dylan gives the ball one of his almighty kicks. The ball rises and rises. It's got the distance. It starts to dip. The goalie sees it. He scrambles backwards. He's not going to make it. He doesn't make it! He ends up in the back of the net with the ball!

A stunned silence. Nobody can believe it, apart from Dylan. He sprints to Sha and hugs him. The rest of the team follow.

The crowd start cheering. A lot more people are rooting for Sha's team than Eddie's.

Eddie is on the pitch, shouting at the ref. "No goal ref! We wasn't ready! That's bollocks!" Dave joins in, as does Eddie's team, and the parents too.

It is a funny thing, arguing with the ref. Have you ever seen a ref change his mind after he has given a goal, unless his linesman has a word? No. So why do people do it?

Eddie takes his anger out on the players. "Hilly, sort that idiot of a goalkeeper out! And liven up, the rest of you wankers!"

The game settles down a bit. The A-team are on the attack, again and again. They hit the bar twice, then the crossbar. Sha's team start moving up a bit, and try and catch them offside. It's working, and frustrating Eddie and his team. The half-time whistle blows.

In the dressing room, Sha and his team are ecstatic. As for Wayne, he is on a different planet!

"We can do it, we can, we can fucking do it. Sorry, I mean flipping do it."

Sha hugs Dylan. "Great spot, Dylan."

"Freddie told me before kick-off, to look and see if it was on."

"Well done son, what made you think of that?"

"Dad, that goalie and Hilly argue all the time. I've noticed it before in training."

The whole team group hug. "No matter what happens, we had our half!" screams out Sha.

Eddie's dressing room is a little less calm. He is giving his team talk. "They are shit. We are the best team in the county. If we lose this game, we'll be a laughing stock, not only in the footballing sense, but half the village is watching. Get out there and score ten goals. Now go on, go!" He gestures dismissively towards the door.

The game restarts. Play takes the same pattern as before. Attack after attack from the A-team. They get a corner. It looks like the goalkeeper is going to get the ball, but he gets fouled, and the ball slips into the net. The ref gives the goal, and Eddie's team go wild.

Hilly turns to Freddie. "Just like your dad. A loser."

Freddie makes to go after him. Dylan jumps in. "Calm down, we haven't lost yet."

Freddie kicks off and passes it to Dylan. Hilly isn't switched on yet. He's taking applause from his goalkeeper. They high five each other. Dylan plays the ball in front of Freddie, who runs onto it and strikes it perfectly. Hilly turns and sees the shot coming. It's low and hard. He tries to deflect it, but misses. The goalkeeper is unsighted and doesn't see it. Goal!

This time, Sha's team don't go mad celebrating. The game isn't over yet. Eddie is still shouting the odds, but no one is listening.

Two fantastic goals from Sha's team. It just goes to show, you can teach as much technical stuff as you want, but sometimes you just have to play what is in front of you.

The game kicks off again. There can't be much time left. Some clever work from Sean puts Hilly through on goal. The B-team has moved up for the offside, but he has slipped through. The goalie comes charging out. Hilly goes down as he tries to pass the keeper. Is it a foul? It depends on which team you believe. Hilly gets up and winks at Freddie. The ref sends the keeper off. It's inside the box. Penalty. The crowd are booing; they know exactly what has happened.

Martin, the old keeper, pulls on the keeper's shirt. Freddie walks over and pats him on the back. Hilly is taking the penalty. He spots the ball. Freddie walks past Hilly and has a word, "Miss this, and you'll be the biggest loser this town has ever seen."

Hilly pushes him away. He takes three strides back, moves a bit to the left, and starts his run. He catches it beautifully, but it sails just over the bar. The final whistle blows. Hilly sinks to his knees, holding his head. Eddie seethes on the touchline, spitting venom, and telling Dave to fuck off when he says something meant to be consoling.

The crowd go mental! Everybody loves an underdog. Freddie runs to his family. He jumps into his dad's arms, then hugs his mum and Louise. Jessica appears. He hugs her too, and gives her a kiss, then realises what he has done. She smiles, and kisses him back.

Some of the A-team players come up and congratulate Sha and the boys. It was a nice touch. Eddie is seen storming off, remonstrating with his son. You wouldn't want to be in that house tonight.

"What a day!" said Wayne. Four months ago, you'd have laughed if someone told you that was going to happen! That was bloody brilliant!"

Finale

The cup final day arrived. They had made it.
Not much to say really. They lost five-nil, but they didn't really mind.
They had already had their day, as every dog does.
The semi-final day was that day.

THE END

Ruby Soho

By

Kevee Lynch

Ruby and Polly

The song 'Ruby Soho' by Rancid was playing on the stereo in Ruby's car. It was a song she often played. Her favourite song. Some years back, she had changed her name by deed poll to Ruby Soho.

She was a fifty-year old lady, who carried her age very well. She still liked to dress in black, something she had done from when she first got into punk, at the young age of fourteen. She was dark-haired and very petite. Her daughter Polly was with her. She was thirty-five, and she wore more colourful clothes, but still liked a lot of the punk attitude that her Mum had to this day.

They were just popping to the shops, and both singing along to 'Ruby Soho.' It wasn't really a car they were driving, although it had five seats. It was one of those double-cab pickup trucks. Ruby loved the safety aspect of a four-wheel drive truck with nudge bars front and back.

They pulled into the car park of the supermarket, and as luck would have it, a car was just pulling out of a parking space. Ruby steered the truck straight in. Another driver had seen the car pulling out, and was just about to reverse in, but Ruby had sneaked in first. Next thing, the driver of the other car was tooting his horn, not one of those nice, short double toots, to say 'thanks', but the long, 'keep your finger on it' toots that go on and on, to say 'I'm pissed off'.

Ruby and Polly didn't get excited by such behaviour, and carried on talking as they got out of the car. The driver however, wasn't so calm, and wound down his window. "What do you think you are doing, you stupid bitch? This is my space! I saw it first!" Ruby and Polly just ignored the insults and continued on their way, which infuriated the driver even more.

"Move your fucking car, now."

Ignoring people who have a bit of road rage can make them get over-excited. The man parked his car in front of the truck. He got out and locked his car, while muttering "That will teach them" under his breath.

Ruby and Polly grabbed a trolley and entered the shop. "Mum, why didn't you say anything to that man? It's not like you."

"Sometimes it's best if I keep my mouth shut. I don't know what gets into some people. Guys like that get behind the wheel of their flash cars, and turn into somebody else. I think they call it 'Little Man Syndrome'."

Polly was in agreement with her mum, "Ha-ha, I get it! A bit like 'big car, small dick syndrome.'"

"Something like that, Polly."

They carried on filling the trolley, walking up and down various aisles, and chatting away about the big party that night. Ruby was celebrating her fiftieth birthday.

Something had been bugging Polly. "Mum, why have you invited so many people tonight that you don't really like? You don't need them to come, so why bother?"

"It will be good, Polly. All my real friends are coming, plus the other lot. They bullied me at school, and constantly took the piss out of me, and I think tonight is the chance for a bit of payback. They are so obsessed with money, and the 'I'm so much wealthier than you' attitude. They haven't got *half* what they think they have. Life is just one big false front."

"So why invite them?"

"Because it is my night, and they are going to hate it, and I'm going to love that."

The man from the car park walked past them and said "You'll have to wait for me to finish my shopping before you can move that shit heap of a truck you are driving. I'm parked in front of you, and I'm not in any rush to get home."

He walked on, smirking. Ruby had to grab Polly, who was starting to go after him.

"Leave it Polly. It's not worth it."

Polly conceded, but couldn't help thinking that it was unlike her mum not to stand her ground. 'Must be because she is fifty today.' They got to the checkout, and unloaded the trolley. The young checkout girl put the shopping through the till and they packed it away into some bags.

"That will be £147.50, please. And may I say, I love your hair and outfit."

Ruby often got complimented on her look these days, and she often thought to herself that she was born thirty years too early. On the other hand, if her generation hadn't started sticking up for themselves back in the day, we could all still be wearing frilly dresses and three-piece suits. She took the compliment, and thought 'What a nice young girl.'

They thanked the girl, headed out to the car park, and sure enough, the guy had his car parked right in front of them. Polly was not very happy, "For Christ's sake, that dickhead has parked in front of us! We need to get home for the party. How are we going to get out?"

"Just get in the truck Polly. You can't legislate for twats in this world."

They put the shopping in the back of the truck, and got in. Ruby started the truck up. "The beauty of having an old truck like this with nudge bars and a massive tow bar, is that you don't have to wait for anyone." With that, she slammed it into reverse, and it flew straight backwards, into his precious car.

"Like you say, we have a party to go to, and this will teach him to be such a jerk."
She pulled forward a bit, and then gave it another go in reverse. "Plenty of room to get out now!" They both

gave out a loud cheer. "I might be fifty, Polly, but you should know me better than that."

Polly just smiled, and then nodded. Yes, she should have known her mum would not put up with the situation. They passed the driver as they left the car park, and they both gave him the finger. He dropped his bags, and ran to his car. It was in a sorry state, and he was incensed. "Fucking bitches!" He started kicking his own car, while still screaming "Fucking bitches!"

A police car just happened to be driving past, and saw what was going on. The police officer pulled into the car park, and stopped behind the man. The officer wound down his window. "What seems to be the trouble sir?"

"Them two bitches in that truck backed into my car and drove off. They stole my parking space, so I blocked them in, and now they have fucking wrecked my car!" He was still kicking his car.

The officers glanced around the car park, but couldn't see a truck. "I can't see a truck, Sir. Were there any witnesses to this alleged accident?"

The man stopped kicking his car and turned to the officers. He tried to speak calmly, almost spelling it out. "The truck has driven off, and I don't know if there are any fucking witnesses!" He had lost the plot again, turning and booting his car, and screaming.

The police officer stayed calm, not wanting to escalate the situation. "Sir, all I can see is you kicking a car. If it is your own car, may I suggest that with no witnesses, and only us two watching you damage your own car, it's not going to help you with an insurance claim, now is it?"

"Don't fucking start on me, you pair of twats! Do your job, and go and arrest them two bitches!"

Both officers had had enough. They got out of the police car, and told him firmly to calm down. This really wasn't going to work. He gave the car one almighty last boot, and told the police officers to "Go fuck yourselves!"

This *did* get a reaction. He got his head slammed on the bonnet, and was then duly handcuffed, while having his rights read to him. It wasn't turning out to be a good morning. Perhaps he should have gone to anger management classes, as his wife had suggested just before she left him.

Syd

Syd and Siobhan lived in a big house on the posh side of town. He had done well for himself in life. He was a bit dodgy, but he liked to think that was part of being a good business man. He may have trampled over a few people to get where he was today, but he had been doing that since school.

He was a big lad at school, and called the shots. A good sportsman, a good-looking chap, and with pretty wealthy parents, he had it all. These days, his looks had escaped him, but he was fairly happy. The strange thing was that tonight he was going to the birthday party of the one girl he had really wanted at school, but the one girl who would have nothing to do with him.

He had got a bit over-amorous with her on the way home from school once, but once only. They had been walking through the park. Well, *she* was. He just caught her up, and tagged along. When they got to a quiet spot, he grabbed her and tried to kiss her. She was a little taken aback at first, so he proceeded to touch up her breasts. Only to be met with one almighty kick in the nuts, and a punch round the face. That was it. He never mentioned it again, and neither did she. His pride had been hurt by the fact that she didn't want him, so it was best to let it go. Over the years at school it had been forgotten, and she was a nothing, really. He still wondered if it would have been better if he'd made a different approach. No, she was a saddo. He was better off the way things had turned out.

Siobhan had met Syd at school. She wasn't sure she loved him. She probably never did, but his mother and father were rich, and he was always going to do well. She was also popular at school, part of 'The Bitches'. Yes, they actually called themselves that. You get them in every school, a group of about five to fifteen girls, who think they are something they are not. Usually good-looking, to be honest, and they might let a not so good-looking one into the group if she has something to offer, like her mum and dad own a ski chalet, or something like that. It's always good to let a bit of an ordinary one in, to make you look better, as well as someone you can all feel sorry for!

Siobhan and The Bitches had ruled that school, and made it a misery for plenty, including Ruby. That was the odd thing about getting invited to this party. She couldn't work out why. Still, Janice and Chantelle were coming, so that was a third of the original nine Bitches, and the main three.

The doorbell rang, and Syd went to answer it. He didn't rush. He couldn't, anyway, as he had a massive beer belly these days, and his joints weren't good. Even his hair has disappeared. Old age was definitely sneaking up on him. Siobhan was in the kitchen, over the other side of the house. He opened the door and shouted out. "It's Janice!"

You would have thought Janice was ten years younger than him. She had no husband or kids, and kept herself to herself. She was often travelling the world, and generally taking it easy.

As she entered, Syd gave her a big kiss on the lips, while at the same time putting his arms around her and squeezing her bottom. "That arse is holding up well for your age."

She brushed him off. "Get off Syd. You have lipstick on your face now." She wiped it off.

Siobhan came into the hallway. "Syd stop molesting my school mate! Hello Janice, you look fab, as always." Janice still had her slim, elegant, young look, whereas Siobhan had let herself go a bit. She looked her age, if not older. The pounds had crept on slowly but surely over the years, not through eating, but just the amount of alcohol she consumed. There wasn't a day went by when a bottle or two of wine didn't get drunk.

Janice always acted as a kind friend though. "You're looking good this morning. Love that dress! Where did you get it?"

'Thanks Janice. It's a new designer, very up and coming. You know me, bit of a trendsetter."

Syd was still hovering about. "Yeah, probably cost me about five hundred quid!"

Syd always had the knack of saying the wrong thing, and Janice duly told him "You want your wife to look beautiful, don't you Syd?"

Siobhan gave a little twirl. "I've still got it, haven't I, Syd?"

He didn't answer that question, instead opting for "I need to pop to the office for a bit. Catch you all later." With that, he was off.

Siobhan and Janice headed for the kitchen. Siobhan went to put the kettle on, then did an about face, and grabbed an opened bottle of wine and a couple of glasses. "Let's have half a glass. Get us in the mood for tonight." She promptly poured two full glasses.

"What about this party Janice? I can't believe Karen has invited us!"

"You have to call her Ruby now, Siobhan. Remember, she changed her name years ago."

"I know. What was that all about? She's always wanted to be either something or someone else. The clothes she used to wear at school! I think she thought she was Siouxsie Sioux, out of the Banshees."

"More like Poly Styrene out of X-Ray Spex, with those braces she used to wear!"

Kids can be terrible at school. They say there's no worse place than the playground for bullying. These two hadn't lost their nasty edge. Some people never do. "Well she never really integrated at school."
"Chantelle hated her and so did I. You were the only one out of our lot that talked to her."

"That was me playing clever. Some of the boys surprisingly fancied her. I thought being nice would make me look a bit caring. I'm sure your Syd had a bit of a thing for her before you came along."

"No, he said he used to flirt a bit, to see if he could break the ice queen down." She took a slurp of her wine. "You know he only had eyes for me, Janice."

"That might have had something to do with you giving him a blow job once a week behind the bike sheds!"

Siobhan found this amusing. "Easiest way to keep a man happy! If all the blood's in his cock, there's none left in the brain. So if you want anything off them, it's a good time to ask."

"You're terrible, Siobhan!"

"Yep, but I got what I wanted! Big house, big car and a big salary of his to spend. The only problem is I have a grumpy, big balding husband to go with it!"

"A small price to pay then, for what you have. Getting back to Ruby, has she moved? The party is at some posh address tonight. Can't be her house, she used to live in that right little hovel."

"You know what I think Janice, she's probably the cleaner, and they have let her use the garage for the night. Or she has learnt how to give a good blow job!"

Janice got up. "Maybe you're right. Right, I have to go. Got something to do before the party. I'll catch you later." Janice headed towards the door, and Siobhan followed her. They kissed at the door, and Janice walked to her car, still talking. "What time is Chantelle arriving"?

"Not too sure. She was finishing a modelling job in LA, then jumping on a plane. She should be en route now. She won't want to miss the party, rub Ruby's face in it a bit about her jet-setting life style. I wonder if that other weirdo Gez is coming. He was always hanging about with Ruby."

"Probably all the old weirdos will be there. Right, I'll see you later Siobhan."

"OK see you later. Do you really think I look good in this dress?"

"Of course you do darling."

Janice shut the car door, and waved goodbye, while muttering under her breath, "If you like looking like the back end of a bus."

Home

Ruby and Polly had arrived home, and were unloading their shopping. A taxi pulled up behind them, and two men got out.

Polly shouted "Dad!" she turned to Ruby. "They're early." She ran over and gave Gez, her father, a big cuddle, and then did the same to Peter, who she referred to as 'uncle.'

Gez walked over to Ruby and they embraced and kissed. He stepped back and surveyed the property. "You finally did it Ruby, all on your own!"

"Yep, I did! It did help, the fact that I had my best mate doing so well, and showing me that anything was possible." Peter walked over. "Peter, you *are* looking sharp!" He gave a knowing grin, then grabbed Ruby and squeezed her. "When did you guys fly in?", asked Ruby.

"Oh it was yesterday afternoon. Peter booked a hotel for us up in Soho. We had a crazy night, went to a club. It was filled with all sorts of people. Not the usual crowd at all. Everyone was hammered though, good night. We nearly called you, Ruby, you would have loved it."

"I was up to my eyeballs, cooking for tonight."

They headed towards the house, gathering all the shopping and cases. They dumped the shopping in the kitchen, and Peter and Polly headed upstairs. They had a gift for Polly, and Peter was eager to show her.

Ruby turned on the iPod dock, and a bit of old-school punk started playing. Some people like to come home from a day out and sit in silence to unwind. Others reach for the remote and turn the television on. Ruby always put music on, either her stereo or the radio.

Gez fondly remembered, "You never change, Ruby, you still love this music."

"Well, John Peel kept listening to punk, right up until he died. If it was good enough for him, it's good enough for me."

Gez was in awe of the house. "Ruby, the house is fantastic! This must have cost a fortune! It's *so you* though!"

It certainly *was* Ruby's house. It wasn't overrun with brass and gold fittings. It was modern, but the colours were deep and moody, not your middle-of-the-road magnolia. The kitchen was different, all gloss white, with black trim. The floor was polished tiles in a black and white chequered pattern, very reminiscent of the 2-Tone music era. Ruby loved her punk, but also ska, and especially bands from the 2-Tone label. "It's all paid for, every part of the house and everything in it. Can you believe that?"

"You done good girl."

"We both did."

"You got what you always wanted Ruby. You got independence."

"Gez, a long time ago, you gave me what I always wanted. Someone to love and look after. You gave me Polly. That's what I always wanted, and you and Peter were always looking over my shoulder for me. I was just a bit stubborn. I should've let you in more." She cupped his face with her hands. "I'll always love you, Gez."

"You never judged me, Ruby."

"What was there to judge? I knew you better than anyone. Christ, Gez, you used to wear more eyeliner than me when we went out, and your clothes were so well co-ordinated."

"I *did* used to cake it on. Still do, on special occasions. I love you too Ruby. You are my soulmate."

"And you mine. Enough now, I need to get on. You can give me a hand with the salad." Gez walked up to the iPod, and selected one of his favourite bits of upbeat ska music, the Sko-Mads, with 'Born To Fuck Up.' They had a bit of a dance before getting on with the food preparation.

The story of Ruby and Gez went back a long way. They both struggled to fit in to secondary-school life. Ruby's mother had died when she was very young. Cancer had got hold of her for a short, but torrid time. Ruby's dad really struggled with this for a long while. Ruby and her dad moved in with her grandmother. She loved

Ruby, and would spoil her rotten. Her dad just lost his way. He started drinking, and then not coming home some nights. He finally sorted himself out after a few years, and was moving forward. Ruby then lost her grandmother, which was another massive blow. Her dad knuckled down and threw himself into work. This left Ruby with a lot of time on her own. She took on the role of mother, cooking and cleaning. By the time she reached secondary-school, her dad had met someone else, and moved her into the family house. Ruby didn't want to be at home too much, and neither did she want to be at school. A lot of her time was spent at Gez's.

Gez only had a mum. His abusive father was long gone, and good riddance! Gez wasn't your big bully type at school. He loved music, and dressed a bit alternative. He had gravitated towards Ruby, a kindred spirit. They were not romantically involved in any way, just mates doing everything together. They both loved punk music, the alternative clothes that went with it, and left-wing politics. They were living their dream, not at school, but away from all that bullshit. Their other big love was cider! It was the drink of alternative youth. They had dabbled a bit in drugs, as most kids do, but who needed drugs when you could buy three litres of cider for fifty pence? When they were fifteen, they got so drunk that the unthinkable had happened. They woke up both realising that they had had sex. It was a one off. They loved each other, but not in that way. Ruby wasn't looking for a relationship. She wanted to be independent, and Gez was struggling with his sexuality. The thing was, Ruby was pregnant. She decided she wanted the baby. She needed someone to look after. Gez would stand by her, but she knew it was unfair. It wasn't a path he wanted to go down. They would tell no one who the father was. Gez vowed to stand by her though, for the rest of his life.

In the kitchen, they were both getting on with the food preparation, while jumping around to the ska that Gez had selected, which was booming out of the speakers. Gez was on the salad, chopping away, mostly in time with the music. Ska has an infectious beat, and if you have succumbed to it early in life, it never leaves you. Now, there's nothing wrong with slow, moody ballads if that is your thing, but ska just picks you up. It's hard not to find yourself jumping about.

"Have you invited the three moronic bitches?", asked Gez.

"Yes, bitches one and two are coming, not too sure about bitch number three, Chantelle."

"I saw her recently at a fashion shoot in LA. She was modelling clothes I designed. I thought it hilarious! She didn't see me, I kept out of the way."

Ruby was intrigued, and wanted to know more. "What's she like? Is she still a bitch?"

"Oh yes! Major bitch, *and* major coke head. She still loves the attention, but she was definitely hitting the coke at 10am in the morning. You would've laughed though! She's modelling middle-aged stuff now."

"Cardies and sweaters?"

Gez was laughing out loud as he managed to say, "And control pants! *Not* a pretty sight! What about the other two? What are they up to?"

"I saw Siobhan the other day in town. That's when I invited her. A pair of control pants wouldn't do her a lot of good these days, though. She was *so* horrible to overweight people at school, being like a stick herself. She has definitely changed! I think she still thinks she's a size ten, judging by the clothes she was wearing. As for Janice, she has a nice flat, and plenty of money. Not sure how she gets all that. Rumours are rife that some wealthy bloke keeps her well-looked after. She looks vacant though, do you know what I mean? When you look in her eyes, there's nothing there. No emotion, no inquisitiveness, just coldness. Very odd, I think she just wants to be loved."

Gez, having been away for a long time, liked an update from Ruby. Ruby wasn't exactly seeing many of the old school crowd, but she had her ear to the ground, and picked up the odd bit here and there.

Gez wanted to know about his three old friends. "Whatever happened to *our* crew? Are they coming?"

"Oh yes, Half A Man."

"Blimey! Half A Man! How's he doing?"

"Still about four foot two, shag anything that moves, and still drinks like a fish. Lurch is coming too. After living in a squat for years, he managed to save up and buy a house. He soon got that rented out, and bought a few more. The thing with Lurch is, he charges rich people to live in his houses, and with the money coming in, he bought an old Manor House, renovated it all, and now runs it as a hostel. He's a good lad, that one, he's like a modern day Robin Hood. Robs the rich to give to the poor. The funny thing is, he lives on the top floor of the hostel. He loves it! Then of course there's Wurzel."

'Wurzel! He must be still gardening, isn't he?"

"Yep, only went and landed a job as head-gardener up at some mansion house! He was always going to do well, that one. He knew everything about plants. Apparently he tidied himself up for the interview, and the lady of the house took a bit of a shine to him. So he only landed a property to live on in the grounds! He took on the whole role of maintaining two hundred and fifty acres. Then he sacks everyone, brings his own team in, and gets paid a fortune to look after everything. The bloke who owns it is always away on business, usually with his PA. So, the story goes, the Lady of the Manor comes on to him big time, for about six months. One day, she phones him and asks him to come up the house. Her wardrobe door has fallen off. He pitches up an hour later, no sign of her, so he goes up to sort the door. She comes out of the en suite, all made up, with only sexy black underwear and stockings on. She tries to make out she forgot he was coming. Wurzel is a bit embarrassed, says he's sorry, and so on. She starts asking him what he thinks of her new underwear? Poor old Wurzel said he was as red as a beetroot, but at the same time he's getting aroused, and the next thing he knows, she's grabbed hold of his manhood, and he is in there like a rabbit down a burrow!"

Gez was enjoying this story. "Crikey! That's an awkward situation, what with his job and everything!"

"That's the best bit, she comes round to his the next day, all worried that her husband might find out, and sling her out on the streets. *He's* worried he could lose the house *and* his job, so they agree to keep it quiet, which would suit them both. The best bit is, neither of them want a romantic relationship, but she turns round and asks if he's up for some more nookie every now and again. Her husband is apparently hopeless in bed. Wurzel was like, 'Hmm ... no strings attached hardcore sex every now and again.' He thought it was his birthday! He likes to think he is being used by the Lady of the Manor, and getting paid for it. She even told him to up his prices by ten percent! Happy days, or what?"

"All the lads have done well, Ruby. I would never have thought that at school, us five amounting to much at all; we were all a bit soft in those days."

"I forgot to say Half A Man not only shags anything that moves, and drinks like a fish, he also invented some app that took off big time. Made an absolute killing! Never tells anyone. You'd think he didn't have two pennies to rub together. He likes it that way, no false friends jumping on his wealth."

Polly came into the kitchen with Peter. She was wearing a stunning new dress and shoes. Gez took her hand, and made her do a twirl. "Your Mum done good Polly; what a beautiful young woman!"

Polly dragged him off. "Come on, I'll show you the party room." She led him through into a massive room, all set up with lights, disco, and even a stage area, with instruments ready to play. "Did you sort the band, Dad?"

"I did indeed. Your mum's going to freak out!" Polly gave him a big hug. This was going to be a night to remember!

Chantelle

Chantelle had arrived at Heathrow Airport. She hated airports, especially the bits where you had to mingle with the lowlifes, passport control, and the dreaded baggage carousel. She just wanted to get home. It had been a hectic trip. She didn't even have a luxury cab booked to pick her up. The unthinkable was happening. She had to queue, like everyone else. She had just dialled Janice's number, when a cab arrived. She was quite pleased. She wouldn't have to talk to the driver now. She just gestured with her hands for him to pick up and load her bags. She was giving it the 'I'm on the phone' bit. He just loaded the stuff and opened the door for her. He knew this type; they couldn't *possibly* open a cab door themselves!

She was in full flow now, with Janice. "Yes, I've just arrived. I'm heading to St. Albans now." She shouted at the driver "Town Centre, St. Albans." Then she continued with Janice. "Yes, my parents are away, so I'm staying at their house. I'm looking forward to meeting up tonight! You can come round for pre-drinks. I think I'll need it. I can't *believe* she is having a 50th party! I mean who wants to celebrate that?" The cab driver was having a sneaky look at Chantelle's legs in the rear view mirror. She caught him doing so, and moved her legs so that he could see a little bit more. The poor bloke took his eye off the road, and then had to brake hard, as the car in front had slowed down. Chantelle gave him some abuse. "You've had a good look, now keep your eyes on the road!" She carried on with Janice "Jesus, Janice what is it with men? They see a bit of leg, and their brain stops working!"

The cabby was gesturing his apologies, doing the hand shrug, as if to say 'What did I do?' Chantelle switched him off. She couldn't be doing with him now. She was engrossed in her conversation with Janice.

"You got that lover of yours to ditch his wife yet?" There was no reply from Janice, just a pause. "You say you don't want him, but one of these days he's going to want someone a bit younger than you. What are you going to do then? I hope you have been stashing some of that money." Another pause. "Alright Janice, no more lectures, I'll see you tonight about 7pm."

She put the phone down, and started rummaging through her bag. The cab driver scrutinised her in the mirror, and had to ask "Excuse me, but don't I know you from somewhere? You look very familiar."

Now, although Chantelle couldn't be bothered with people who she thought were beneath her, she was just like most celebrities; she loved being recognised. She had positively craved being one of the popular clique at school, and this had carried on into her modelling career. She thought herself very successful. The jobs had dried up a bit, and she seemed to be getting older-type work, but she was still earning the bucks. She needed to. After a string of rich boyfriends, she had found herself on her own. That was bad enough, but having to pay for your own things, and drugs, was putting a massive dent in her finances. She knew someone would come along soon to scoop her off her feet. If Mister Cabby thought it was him, he was very much mistaken. She would enjoy the adoration from him though. "Well, I *am* a model, so you may have seen me in something. Or on the television."

"I knew it! What sort of things do you do?"

She loved this bit the best. "Oh, I've been on the catwalk in Paris, London and New York, and I do a lot of high class magazines in America."

The cabby nodded his head in agreement "Yep, must've seen you in the magazines."

Chantelle liked the upper hand. "I don't think so, deary. I'm not in the sort of magazines that you buy. Penthouse or Playboy aren't my thing. I don't do that sort of modelling."

The cab driver now apologised. "I am sorry I didn't mean them sort of mags. I don't buy those sorts of things."

She was cruel. She liked to see people squirm a little. She undid her seatbelt, and took her jacket off. She pushed her chest out, and sucked in her waist a bit. She *really* loved herself, and she was letting him take it all in. He was your typical cabby. He wanted to keep the chat going. He had decided this was his last fare for the day, as St. Albans was literally up the road from where he lived. "How did you get yourself into modelling?"

If she *must* talk to him, talking about herself was the best option. "It was a while back. I got noticed just after I left school. I did a few photo shoots, to build a portfolio, then got offered some work in catalogues, and it took off from there. The rest, as they say, is history."

"What catalogues did you do?"

"Littlewoods, Freemans."

"Freemans! My mum used to get that!"

She wanted him to ask about other things. 'Catalogues' was just the start of a long list she could rattle off. "Well, like I said, a long time ago."

"I don't mind telling you, I used to *love* looking at those catalogues as a young lad. Well, the lingerie bit." He studied her face again. "You must have been in the lingerie bit. That must be where I've seen you. It must be, because that is the only bit I used to look at, apart from the Scalextric."

She wasn't enjoying the attention now, or the thought of this man ogling all over her in the semi-nude. "Like I said, a very long time ago."

The cabby's mood had dramatically changed. He was like a little schoolboy. "Yeah, I remember you now! Me and you go back a *long* way darlin'! I used to take you to bed! Not in person, if you know what I mean." He was enjoying this. The shoe was on the other foot now. "Yep, you were my favourite, darlin'! I definitely remember you now. Bloody hell! I was only a kid. You've aged well, you must be over fifty. Who'd have thought it? I have my very own catalogue girl in the cab! I should be embarrassed!"

'This hasn't gone according to plan', thought Chantelle. She slipped her jacket back on and pulled out a book to read. It was called 'The Dark Secrets of an Outsider'. She slipped down in her seat a bit to avoid any more eye contact with the driver. "Just drive. Get me home."

The cabby was having his revenge, and she wasn't gloating any more. "I hear that's a good book. Women all over the world are reading that. They say it's about keeping a man, and looking and staying slim. For the older woman. I suppose at your age, it is difficult to keep the weight off."

Chantelle was counting the minutes. "If you don't mind."

"No, I don't mind. I don't mind at all." He shook his head from side to side, chuckling. "You wouldn't credit it, would you? My childhood sweetheart in the back of the cab! Wait till I tell the lads!"

Ruby's House

Back at Ruby's house, preparations were nearly complete. The music was blaring out in the main party room, which bordered on the size of a hall. The stage lights were flashing in tune with the bassline of the music. The PA system was very professional-sounding, and better than you get in many local pubs. Ruby often wondered why venues didn't lay out a bit of money for a good sound system. There was nothing worse than distorted speakers being overdriven. The place was well-decorated, with banners telling everyone she was fifty. Age didn't really bother her. She still felt eighteen. Age is a state of mind. If you thought you were too old to try something else, then you probably were. How many fifty-year olds were counting the days to retirement? Try something different every year. Your next could be your last.

She entered the kitchen. Polly, Peter and Gez were busying themselves hanging a few more banners. They didn't stop. They were on a mission to get the last one up. Ruby looked at the three of them, all dressed up. These three were her best friends. No malice in them, just love for each other, and for her. The rollercoaster ride of life had always brought them closer together. Ruby's life could have run a very different course, if she had let things get on top of her. She chuckled to herself, thinking back to her old bedroom. On the top shelf of the bookcase at the end of her bed, was a glass. The glass was always there. It only came down once a week, when she tidied her room. She would wash it, and fill it half-full, and put it back. When she woke in the morning, the first thing she would always see was the half-full glass. It would set her up for the day. Some would say it was a half-empty glass. That was the point of it. She would always fill it half-full. You don't fill anything half-empty, do you? Maybe it was odd, but she still kept the glass at the end of her bed, on a different bookcase, and today she had filled it to the top. It was the first time she had ever done that. She felt today that her life was complete. Nothing anyone could say or do would make her feel any different.

She gazed upon the three, Gez, Polly and Peter. They had finished, and were admiring their work. She was still admiring their clothes. "Thanks guys, the place looks excellent! As do you three!"

"Not bad," replied Polly. "Hey Mum, how many did you say are actually coming tonight? I know you invited loads"

"About one hundred and fifty, I think. Mind you, it could be just us three!"

Peter was quite surprised by this. "One hundred and fifty! Christ, Ruby, you usually keep yourself to yourself! Do you *know* that many people?"

"We'll find out tonight, wont we?"

Gez was scanning the room. "What's with all the TV screens, Ruby?"

"Now, *that* is a story! I wanted to film the party for a keepsake. As you say, I don't normally have many people around. I had cameras fitted all over the house.

I can select any room, and stick it on the screen. Look." She picked up the remote, pressed different numbers, and different rooms came up. "I can also bring up what was recorded earlier. Look." This time, it showed the party room being set up earlier in the day.

"Have you become a stalker, Mum?"

They all laughed. Ruby wanted to know one more thing. "Who is the band tonight?" No-one was letting on, and it was beginning to annoy her. "Come on, it's my party! All I know is that it is a ska/punk band. What's the big secret?" Nobody was going to let on, however, so Ruby changed the subject. "You all look great, anyway! Gez, in your designer suit and trilby. You, Peter, in your two-tone suit, and Polly, with your flash new dress."

"And *you* look great too Mum, all in black. Fred Perry, mini-skirt and DMs. Your classic combo! Guys, how can she look so good in the same clothes she's been wearing for nigh on forty years?"

"She's still got it", said Gez. "Bloody gorgeous!"

They all had a group hug and a squeeze. The doorbell rang. The first guests must be arriving. Ruby took a deep breath. "Right, let's do this!"

She headed to the door, took another deep breath, and flung it open. "Is this where the party's at, you old fucker? Give us a cuddle before you get too old, and smell of piss." It was her old friend, Half A Man. She gave him a massive cuddle, picked him up, carried him through the doorway, kicked the door shut, then put him down. He was straight off to the kitchen. "Come on! Let's get this party started!" The doorbell rang again, and Half shouted back at her "You shut the door in Lurch's face! Ha-ha! Forgot to tell you he was behind me!"

'That was a good start, slamming the door in your guest's face', thought Ruby. "Lurch! You made it! Sorry about the door, Half never said you were behind him."

He picked Ruby up. "Wouldn't have missed it for the world!"

A few more people were in tow, and they all greeted Ruby on the way in. She told Lurch to put her down, but he just wandered towards the kitchen, still carrying her. Half A Man had made it to the kitchen, spotted Gez, and run and jumped on his back. "Gezza, me old mucka!" He gave him a big, sloppy kiss on the cheeks. Gez was pleased to see him. Half A Man could liven any party up. Half jumped down and started dancing. He loved a bit of ska music. Polly brought Half a drink over; well, two actually. Everybody knew Half could down a few. He gave her a big kiss, then walloped the drinks down. He'd hardly broken rhythm, his feet still jiggling away. He was infectious, and everyone started dancing. This could be one long night. Ruby looked on, thinking 'This will definitely be a night to remember!'

Syd and Siobhan

"Hurry up Siobhan! The cab will be here in a moment." What was it with women and getting ready? They always seemed to leave things to the last minute. Siobhan had been getting ready for hours. She knew what time they were going out. Why didn't she plan to be ready an hour early?

Syd liked to be on time or early. Not Siobhan. It was 'lastminute.com' with her.
"I'm coming Syd. Hold your horses!" She entered the room, singing a grand entrance to him "Da-dah! How do I look? Sex on legs, I believe?"

"You look fantastic, dear," he grunted.

"You could at least say it as if you meant it, Syd!"

"I *do* mean it dear. What about me then? Do I look good?"

"Yes."

"Yes, that was very meaningful too."

Old married couples could fall into the familiarity trap. Say the same thing, wear the same thing, eat the same thing. It was a problem familiar to many. Siobhan wasn't in the mood for an argument. Not tonight. She wanted to show the 'happily-married couple' face. "Can we just make this special tonight Syd, please?"

"If you keep your eyes in their sockets, and don't ogle every bloke in there, we might be alright."

"Well, *you* can talk! Maybe you can keep your wandering dick under control, and we might get along fine."

Syd gave her the 'what are you talking about?' expression. "I don't know what you mean."

"Yeah yeah, let's forget it, and try and put on a good front." She had her worries about Syd messing around, and they had been through this many a time.

Syd was thinking 'Here we go again!' "If you were *that* bothered you could always leave." This was the magic touch-paper that always set her off.

"I've told you before. I am not going anywhere. It's *my* house. I've earned it, living with you over the years. *You* want to leave, you leave. But I'll take you to the fucking cleaners!" This was getting out of hand, and they hadn't even got out of the door.

Syd grabbed her, and gave her a hug. "Darling, calm down. I'm sorry."

He could make her so angry, and vice versa. She knew she needed to get it together, tonight of all nights. "Just make sure you don't embarrass me in front of that twat Ruby. I want to be the queen of the ball tonight. You *know* how I like to make her feel inferior. *Please* be the adoring husband, and tell everyone how wonderful I am."

'The tide has turned', thought Syd. She *so* wanted to rub Ruby's face in it that she was pleading with him. This was a very rare occurrence in his household. He remembered way back in time, when he showered her with gifts, so she would have sex with him. It turned from giving gifts, to giving her money. It was like being married to a whore. But the tables were turned tonight. *She* was doing the pleading. He didn't really want sex with her much these days. The love had definitely gone. He sometimes lusted a bit, but not often. When they first got together, he could come home from work, and she would be all ready to jump him as soon as he walked in the door. Looking back, it was probably her just wanting a baby. Who knows? But right here, right now, he felt it was his duty to make her give him a blow job. Why? Because she wanted a big favour off him. "Calm down love. It will be alright." He moved her hand onto his semi-erect member. "Any chance of a quick... ?" He smiled, not finishing the question.

'Typical!' she thought. This night was going wrong before it even started. She had backed herself into a bit of a corner here. She needed Syd to behave, and now he had realised he was in the driving seat. Did he *really* want her to go down on him because he wanted her to, or just because she was giving him shit, but needed him on his 'knight in shining armour' behaviour? It was a lose-lose situation for her now. Refuse, and it wasn't worth going to the party. If he was thirty years younger, she might have enjoyed it. No, maybe thirty years younger and someone else. She braced for the inevitable, and slipped her hands inside his trousers.

The doorbell rang. Syd couldn't believe it. Siobhan was somewhat happier. "Saved by the bell!"

Syd shouted "Alright, coming in a minute!"

"Not *this* minute." She pulled her hand away, zipped up his flies, and gave him a tap on the butt. "Come on, lets go."

Janice and Chantelle

Janice and Chantelle were getting ready for the party, at Chantelle's parents' house. They were a little bit tipsy already. And why not? It was nearly time for the party. Chantelle was just slipping into her dress. Janice was in awe. "Wow! That's a beautiful dress! Where did you get that?"

"It's fabulous, isn't it? Part of the new G&P collection. It's not even out yet. It kind of 'fell into my bag' after my last modelling job."

"It sits so well! Really suits you!"

Chantelle looked down and admired herself. "Being in this line of work, you get a few perks. Designers love to see a top model wearing their gear. And the other perk …" She walked to her bag and pulled out a plastic bag with powder in it, and held it up. "As I was saying, the other perk is drugs. Although I seem to have misplaced most of my stash. It's coke. Do you fancy a line?"

Janice was surprised at Chantelle. "Jesus! Did you bring that through customs? What if you'd been searched?"

Chantelle reached back into the bag and pulled out some very exotic underwear, then some explicit photos of herself wearing it. "I think *this* would've distracted them, don't you?" The photos had been airbrushed a bit. You could see that.

Chantelle was keen to take a line. She cut two lines up on the table, and snorted one up. "Go on Janice, take a hit."

Janice was in two minds. "It's been years."

"Come on, you know you want to! We might be able to get you fixed up with some young man tonight!"

Janice couldn't believe what she was hearing. "At Ruby's party, more like some wino!" She didn't need asking again though, and she snorted a line while Chantelle snorted another for herself. Chantelle now grabbed a bottle of vodka and a couple of shot glasses. She poured the vodka, passed a shot to Janice, and made a toast.

"To old school chums!" Janice gave a nod, and they downed the shots.

They were both thinking about what lay ahead that evening, and Janice piped up. "If nothing else, it will be interesting."

"You're right. I'm looking forward to seeing what a waster Karen, *sorry*, *Ruby*, turned out to be. I don't know why you gave her the time of day. I *hated* that bitch!"

"You always hated her, Chantelle. What did she do to you?"

"This may sound funny, but she was always so fucking *nice*, like she pitied us for the way we were. Then she had the baby, no boyfriend, she was the *last* person you'd have thought would get pregnant. She always dressed in bloody black, just to be different. I just *hated* her. I *bet* she looks rough now. Cranky, old withered face. Spotty and flabby."

"The same, Chantelle."

"What?"

"She looks *exactly* the same. It's unreal!"

"What, stuck in the punk, gothic look, but flabby, right?"

"Yes to the punk look, no to flabby. She doesn't look bad at all. Really looked after herself. Still listening to The Clash and ska, tried to tell me about an American punk band she was into, 'Putrid' or something like that. No, 'Rancid'. That was it, 'Rancid.' Anyway, I'm not looking them up. I'm more into your George Michael."

Chantelle was still reeling from the shock of Ruby not letting herself go. "What a weirdo!"

"What, George Michael?"

"No Janice, not George fucking Michael, Ruby! Have another drink. We've got a party to go to!"

Party

The party was really starting to kick in now. The main room had filled up quite a bit, and the DJ had got the place moving. He knew what this crowd wanted. Old-school punk, new punk, 60's mod and Northern Soul, ska of course, and right now he was banging out some old-school rap. You couldn't beat a bit of Cypress Hill, 'Insane In The Membrane', and judging by the dance floor, it was going down a storm.

As at most parties, the kitchen was one of *the* places to be. The music was still blaring through, the heavy bass tones of rap vibrating the whole house. Half A Man, Lurch, Gez, Peter, Polly and Wurzel were downing shots like they were going out of fashion. Ruby walked in, and Half A Man was straight on her case. "Come on Ruby, get your laughing gear round that!" He gestured to her to take a glass, but she didn't take it.

"I'm good thanks, Half."

Half A Man wasn't listening to that nonsense. He grabbed her hand, made her hold the glass, and then filled it up. He filled everyone's glass up. "Come on, bottoms up, everybody!" They all took the shot, and let out a big cheer. The DJ had started to play House Of Pain's 'Jump Around', a song for any party. Half was jumping up and down before the intro had finished.

Lurch was cracking up. "Oy, Half, if you jump much higher, you might get your head up to everyone else's chest!"

You just *knew* the expletives were going to fly from Half. Polly grabbed his arm. "Come and dance in the room with me, Half. Sod this lot."

Wurzel wanted in on the banter. "Yes Half, see if you can jump high enough to see Polly's chest, you little perv!"

"Piss off the lot of ya! Come on Polly, let's show these old tossers how to dance!"

This was a challenge that Lurch, Wurzel and Peter were up for. They hit the dance floor. Half still had the vodka bottle, trying to fill everyone's glass up. Vodka was going everywhere, except in people's glasses. He was talking to his own hands. "Wey-hey! Steady as she goes!" Who cared, as long as they got a bit in the glass?

Half dashed out of the room, and returned with a couple of bottles of fruit vodka. It was only twenty per cent alcohol, which was a good thing, given the speed at which this lot were drinking. He was still getting most of the vodka down the side of the glass, or on the floor. It was reminiscent of the old TV program 'It's A Knockout', where teams had to fetch a bucket of water, run the gauntlet of obstacles, and pour what was left into a big tank. They used to end up with next to nothing, delivered more or less in the same way that Half was 'delivering' the vodka.

When you get a bit tipsy at a party, does anyone really care? No, not really, and none of this lot seemed to care at all. Lurch was now deliberately moving his glass back and forth as Half was trying to fill it. "Will you hold that fucking glass still, you wanker! I know you're trying to make me look pissed." They were all laughing both *at* Half and *with* him. When people have a few drinks, the language can start to get a bit fruity. We all have times when we try to curb ourselves, but after a few beers, or if we get annoyed, that is when our tongue can run away with us. When the party mood takes us, everything just becomes funnier. Half was dishing out plenty tonight, and also receiving plenty. He loved it. He was with people he could trust. Not shallow acquaintances, but real mates. Gez was still in the kitchen with Ruby. They were busy chatting to people, filling glasses with wine and champagne. The place was getting busier by the minute. The doorbell rang again, and luckily for Ruby, someone was manning the door. It was quite packed, and a bit of a push to get to it. The guy who opened the door said "Good evening, the party is through that crowd somewhere." He pointed towards the crowd.

It was Syd and Siobhan. They looked a bit harassed. They had both expected about twenty people at the most. This place was wall to wall, and it wasn't a small 'two up, two down', it was huge. They pushed through towards the kitchen and Syd caught sight of Ruby. He tapped Siobhan on the shoulder, and pointed out Ruby, and the direction they needed to take.

They finally squeezed through, and Syd put his arms up, ready for a big embrace.

"Ruby, you look great!" She just shook his hand.

"Hi Syd, glad you could make it." She turned to Siobhan "You look lovely, Siobhan." A minor peck on the cheek. 'Well, this is a bit awkward', everyone was thinking.

Siobhan broke the ice a bit. "So many people here tonight! And very lively, to say the least!" She suddenly realised that the guy with Ruby was Gez from school. "Gez, is that you? I haven't seen you for years! Look Syd, it's Gez!" Gez acknowledged that it was him, and there were the same restrained greetings.

Gez didn't like these people. They had treated him, Ruby and the others with contempt at school, and he hadn't forgotten. Siobhan might be many things, but one thing was sure, she was never short of a word or two.

"This is a beautiful house, Ruby! Are you renting it, or have you found a rich man?"

"Neither. It's mine. All paid for."

This was an unexpected reply, and the best Siobhan could muster was "Crikey! Did you win the lottery or rob a bank?"

"Yeah, something like that. Would you guys like a drink?"

Syd held up a bottle of champagne. "Here you go, Ruby, we brought you this as a present. We thought you would only have cider."

Ruby accepted the bottle, and placed it by the other fifty-odd bottles of champagne that she had bought for the party. "Ha! So kind, Syd. I'm not fifteen any more, although Half A Man and his mates *did* bring a couple of crates for old times' sake."

"Half A Man is here? Did you hear that, Siobhan? Half A Man is here!" She had indeed heard it, but chose to ignore it. Her eyes and ears were firmly on the door, waiting for her friends to arrive. Syd continued "I thought he would be dead by now! Where the hell is he?"

"I'm over here"

They all looked confused. They couldn't see him. He emerged from among a group of people. "I'm here, you old tosser, and I ain't dead yet!" He shook Syd's hand, and turned to Siobhan. "Siobhan! Christ, *you've* put on some!"

Gez jumped in quick, and shoved Half away. "Come on Half, this is one of our songs." Catastrophe only just avoided. Siobhan looked a bit shaken, but not stirred.

Gez and Half had got a few paces away, and Half was full of talk. "Here, Gez, I know I'm still Half A Man but she ain't half a woman, more like a woman and a half!" He was laughing at his own jokes. "She was so skinny at school, what happened to her? And Syd the big 'I am' sportsman at school. Has he shrunk or something? Did you see him?"

They both turned back for another glimpse. "Gez man, I'm not kidding! What's happened to his fucking hair? It's all gone! And his belly! It's more like a barrel!"

Gez was struggling to hold it together, witnessing Half A Man's revenge. "Shut up Half, they'll hear you."

"That's made my day, Gez. All the shit I got off him at school. Where's Lurch? Lurch! Lurch! Here, you'll never guess!" Half A Man was running towards Lurch. Gez chuckled, and headed back towards Ruby.

Syd was staring at Ruby, his eyes running up and down, checking her out. It was amazing how some people didn't seem to age. She always had a look about her that Syd liked. That, combined with her attitude, stirred something in Syd. She was 'the one that got away'. At the time, he had brushed it off, thinking she wasn't 'all that' after all. In fact, she *was* all that, and had matured, like a good bottle of wine, getting better with age. "Ruby, you don't look any different at all!"

"Is that a good or a bad thing, Syd?"

"A good thing, I would say! Look at me and Siobhan!" Siobhan looked daggers at him, wondering what he was going to say next. "A good thing for sure, whereas us two ..." he pointed at his own bald head and rolled his hands over his rather large beer belly. He stuttered on, oblivious to the expression on Siobhan's face. "We've put a few pounds on, haven't we darling?" He gave her a little pat on the rear. "Certainly put a few pounds on around here, dear!"

Ruby was enjoying his remarks a lot more than his wife was. Siobhan was wishing she hadn't come tonight. Where were her friends? Gez had joined them again, and Syd was still dishing out the compliments.

"Ah, Gez, I was just saying Ruby has kept herself in shape. You certainly have too, old boy!" He patted his stomach again. "We shall have to get to the gym darling, sooner rather than later." He turned and grabbed a piece of fried chicken off the side, shoved some in his mouth, and continued talking while chewing on the chicken. "As I was saying, we shall have to get in shape."

Janice and Chantelle were just arriving in a taxi. They were both flying high on a mix of coke and drink. Chantelle was chatting away to the cab driver. Unlike her earlier driver, this was a young, fit man. Her snobbery had waned a bit, due to the effects of the drink and drugs. She had spent the whole journey telling him how wonderful her life had been.

Janice had heard it all before many times. It was best to let Chantelle go off on one, and just nod in agreement from time to time. The taxi driver, like a lot of young people, worshipped celebrity status. The way this lady was talking and name-dropping had him on the edge of his seat. This in turn encouraged Chantelle to go on more and more.

Janice found it hard to believe the admiration Chantelle could elicit from people that didn't even know her. Her life sounded fabulous, if you didn't know her, but she knew deep down that Chantelle had never been happy.

No matter what she achieved, it wouldn't be enough. She always wanted what someone else had.

Janice thought about her *own* life. Yes, she was a kept woman, and she got gifts and money a-plenty from her sugar-daddy. She was shrewd though, and had amassed enough money to see her through to her dying days. She liked to holiday, and had travelled a fair bit. Travelling was her escape from her sugar-daddy. He couldn't come with her, because his wife would become suspicious. So she booked plenty of time away. Not too much, though. She didn't want her money to dry up. She had a few flings in the early days, usually young, fit guys. It was a nice change from her man. She liked being in control, but soon realised these young guys didn't really care for her. They just were after her money, in much the same way that she was after her man's money. Maybe she was too guarded, and had low expectations of people. All the years of being at someone else's beck and call had worn her down. Yes, relationships, in her eyes, revolved around money. She almost wanted her man to leave his wife so they could enjoy life as a couple. Would it work? Financially, not really, his wife would clean him out. Also, the thought of being controlled 24/7 was not that appealing. No, she would stay as she was, just try a bit harder to keep her man happy. He had a roving eye. She needed to keep in shape and keep him excited. It was a fair price to pay for what she had.

Chantelle was still going on to the taxi driver, almost leaning in to the front seat with him. They arrived at the party, and bid farewell to the driver. If he was expecting a tip, he didn't get one. Chantelle wasn't throwing her money away, not in *his* direction.

They both stood at the door. Chantelle was excited about the admiration she was going to get from this bunch of losers tonight. Janice had gathered herself, and was thinking that maybe life wasn't too bad. They both knew it would be like being back at school, The Bitches ruling the roost once more, and all the losers looking on longingly, thinking 'if only we were that cool!'

Janice rang the door bell. "Let's get in and party, it sounds quite lively!" The music was blaring out, and you could hear voices enjoying themselves. Chantelle took a step back. "This is a pretty amazing house! It can't be hers!" Was this going to be the night they were hoping for, or could it all go wrong?

The door opened. The place was rammed, and they had to push their way in. Some of the faces looked familiar, but nobody paid them any attention whatsoever. They kept moving forward, hoping to find Siobhan and Syd. They should be here by now. At last, they spotted Siobhan.

'Thank the Lord for that!' thought Siobhan. Now, the tables would turn. "Look everyone, it's Janice and Chantelle!" She jumped on the spot a few times, and clapped her hands excitedly. They finally pushed across the kitchen to reach Siobhan, and they all started hugging and clapping hands.

Gez started to mimic them, and received a dig in the ribs from Ruby. She whispered to him "Pack it in, Gez, I don't want them to go just yet." He gave her a wink, and a peck on the cheek.

After the over-exuberant welcome they had given each other, Chantelle and Janice finally acknowledged Ruby. Janice was first. "Oh, hi Ruby!"

Chantelle did the same. "Hi Ruby, thanks for the invite." It wasn't a very sincere welcome, but then that was to be expected.

Ruby, as always, was her ever-charming self. "Very glad you could make it. It's been a very long time, Chantelle."

"I know, darling. I was just saying the exact same thing to Janice. You haven't changed a bit Ruby, you still look the same. Even your clothes don't change."

There you had it. First dig of the night. It was no more than Ruby was expecting. In fairness, she had thought that just maybe, Chantelle might have changed a bit. But oh no! Thirty seconds in, and she was having a go. Ruby had a wry smile on her face, one which said 'Yeah, start as you mean to go on!'

Siobhan on the other hand, thought that was a great start from Chantelle. She still had the Bitch mentality from school. The night could prove to be a good one after all. Chantelle looked stunning in her dress. She *owned* this party, in Siobhan's eyes. Siobhan just *had* to ask the question. "What a beautiful dress, Chantelle! Where could I get one of those?"

This was what Chantelle wanted. To breeze into the party and be the centre of attention. The dress was to die for! She didn't think they did them in Siobhan's size, but wouldn't let on. She wasn't going to put her mate down in front of Ruby.
"Darling, they haven't hit the stores yet. I'm lucky I'm in the know. I'll try to get you one before they come out."

Gez had been quiet. He leaned over to Ruby, and whispered in her ear. "She's right, Ruby. They *haven't* hit the stores yet. That's one of mine and Peter's designs. She must've stolen it from the shoot I was telling you about."

Chantelle was still giving it out large. "Yes, it's a new design from the G&P Exclusive range. I got given it on a modelling job I was on a week or so ago. Everyone thought I looked so good in it, they decided 'what better advertising than a top model wearing it in public?'"

Gez had to say something. "It really is gorgeous, Chantelle."

"Thanks Gez! How are you, darling? *Your* clothes are pretty sharp too."

"Thank you Chantelle. These are part of a G&P range as well. What a coincidence!"

Chantelle was surprised by this. G&P were a very well-thought of design house. She didn't think Gez would have heard of them, let alone be wearing one of their suits, which cost a fair few pounds. "Did you get yours given to you as well?"

Just the question Gez was fishing for. "As a matter of fact, I did. This is part of the 'Young Men With Attitude' range. That dress is from the 'More Mature Lady' range, if I'm not mistaken. And I don't think I am."

Chantelle was slightly ruffled now. "I don't think so, Gez!" She tried to change the subject. "How is your fashion designing going, Gez? Isn't that what you always wanted to do? I thought you might be wearing your *own* designs like you did at school."

Peter wandered over. He hadn't met Janice and Chantelle before. Well, that wasn't strictly true. He had seen Chantelle on the shoot. "Hi guys, I'm Peter. Gez, are you not going to introduce me?"

"You seem to have introduced yourself. Nevertheless, this is Chantelle and Janice. This is my partner, Peter." Syd, who was just taking a sip of his drink, spurted it out all over the place. "I was going to say business partner Syd, but yes, also my life-partner, as you have so rightly realised."

Syd was wide-eyed. "Jesus, Gez, I never knew you were ... well, you know!"

"Gay. The word is gay, Syd. Don't you remember at school, you used to call me 'homo'?"

"Yes, well, I never thought you actually *were* batting for the other side! It was just a joke."

Ruby couldn't believe this. "Lighten up everybody, it's not the 70s now you know!" What was wrong with people? Live and let live!

Chantelle came across a lot of gay men in her profession. "Business partner, you say? You look like a bit of a fashion guru."

Peter was eyeing up the dress. "Yes, correct."

Chantelle was never one to miss an opportunity to big herself up. "You *must* tell me the name of your little company. I have a lot of contacts in the fashion world. I may be able to put in a good word for you."

At last! The hundred million dollar question that Gez had been waiting all his life to answer! "It's actually called G&P Fashion." This time it was Chantelle who was caught off guard, taking a sip of her drink. She didn't spurt it out, but had trouble gulping it down.

It was one of those spectacular moments. Spectacular for Gez, and Ruby was loving it to see Chantelle trying to comprehend what Gez had just said. Peter was so pleased for his partner; he could see the delight on Gez's face. Chantelle was mortified! The penny was dropping. Ruby thought she'd better keep the conversation going. "Ah, that's lovely. You're all working together! Who would have thought, Chantelle, after all these years, you would be working for Gez!"

The three Bitches were not enjoying this at all. This wasn't how the night was supposed to go. *They* were the ones that made people squirm, not the other way round! They all looked a bit blank.

Things were about to get worse, as Peter chipped in "Not so good you stealing one of our dresses, Chantelle." Boom! Peter had just dropped the bomb! Chantelle's red face said it all. Janice and Siobhan stood, shocked. Chantelle the hero had nicked the dress!

Gez tried to lighten the mood, "Hey, you can keep it, Chantelle. It *does* suit you, you have to agree. Peter, we were aiming for the middle-aged woman market. It definitely fits the market it is aimed at, and everybody here loves it!"

You can go through life thinking you are something special, but you must always be prepared for that one moment. The old saying, 'every dog has its day' was ringing true tonight. Chantelle looked broken. Janice needed to rescue her quickly, and escape the situation. "Come on Chantelle, let's hit the dance floor!" Siobhan knew what Janice was doing. She grabbed Chantelle by the arm and dragged her off. Janice grabbed Syd, who seemed somewhat oblivious to it all, and they were all gone, just like that.

Ruby, Gez and Peter were left with bemused looks on their faces. Ruby was so happy for Gez, more so than for herself. "Well, that was, excuse my language, fucking priceless!"

Gez was a bit gobsmacked, "You couldn't have scripted that!"

They were shaking their heads in disbelief. Ruby had the best idea: "One-nil to the loser brigade! Let's get pissed!"

The evening was going well. Ruby didn't like to be in the spotlight, but tonight was different. It was her party, and she was loving it. The time had flown by. So many people had come to the party, and it seemed that she was genuinely liked. She had really enjoyed the moment with Chantelle getting her comeuppance, and if the party ended this very minute, it would have been a great success, in her opinion. You never knew though, perhaps one of the other Bitches, or Syd, might dig their own grave a bit later.

The Bitches had got over the earlier events, probably due to the drink and the last of the cocaine. The only thing that had been troubling Chantelle was where she could get her next line. Like at most parties, someone would be holding, and she had found that someone about an hour ago. So, at this point in time, she didn't care about much. It would be tomorrow morning when she woke that the realisation of what had happened would hit her.

Wurzel was dancing around the front room with his trousers and shirt off, drinking from a bottle. Lurch was doing selfies with anyone that got within half a metre. Polly was chatting to Ruby in the kitchen, "It's gone well, Mum. Most people seem a little merry." She turned to Half A Man, who was sitting on the floor with his head in his hands, "Are you OK, Half? You look a little the worse for wear?"

Half A Man raised his head, a look of dread in his eyes. "I'm fine. It's just one of those crazy, fucked-up nights. You're never going to believe what just happened!"

Before he had a chance to continue, Chantelle and Siobhan came breezing into the room. Chantelle was completely off her head. "Ruby, what a fantastic party!"

Ruby couldn't make her out. She never could. Does she not remember what happened earlier? Half A Man decided to get out of the kitchen, and go and find Lurch and Wurzel. Ruby decided to talk to Peter and Gez.

Siobhan and Chantelle were checking the kitchen out. The design was not to their liking, but the quality was fantastic. Chantelle spotted a book on the side. "Look Siobhan, it's that book, 'Dark Secrets Of An Outsider'. What a great book." The stupid, excitable hand clapping started.

Siobhan loved the fact Ruby had this book. "Oh, Ruby! Didn't think you'd be into that sort of book! It's a bit risqué!"

"I'm not. It's a pile of shit, written for dickheads, to make a pile of money out of them."

Siobhan and Chantelle both pulled the 'Ooh, get you!' face, and Siobhan added "Well, *you* obviously bought a copy, Ruby. Come to think about it, *you're* a bit of a dark outsider." They both laughed. Not *with* Ruby, but *at* her.

Polly had overheard, and let rip. "Are you *really* that thick?"

Ruby was still the mum though. "Polly," she said, with a warning tone in her voice.

"Well Mum, really! How thick can people be?"

Gez, who had remained quiet up until this point, said "Look around you girls. Look at this place! It cost a fortune!"

Chantelle and Siobhan were both confused, "What do you mean?"

Gez rolled his eyes, thinking 'Give me strength!' "Look at the book. The author's name is R. Soho."

Siobhan didn't get it. "It's what?"

Pete spelled it out. "R. Soho! 'R' being Ruby. Ruby Soho. Do you get it now?"

Chantelle was again taking a swig of wine. This time she didn't gulp. She spat it straight out. "You've got to be fucking joking!" There are moments when you are out enjoying yourself, off your face, and one single thing can sober you up in an instant.

Ruby piped up. "I wrote it to sell copies. Not because I like it, but I knew it would take off, and people are like sheep. Once it takes off, more and more people buy it. I knew people like you two would buy it, so thanks!"

This was another priceless moment for the little people of the world. Gez was beside himself. "You're wearing my clothes, and reading Ruby's book. Fantastic! High five please, Ruby!" High five it was, from Polly and Peter as well.

Chantelle was devastated, to say the least. You could almost take pity on her. The truth of the matter was that she would shrug it off tomorrow, and be telling everyone back in LA what great friends of Ruby Soho she was, and the designers at G& P Fashion. At this moment, she couldn't believe how two no-hopers had done so well.

Siobhan had endured enough. "Come on, Chantelle. I don't know about you, but I'm getting tired. Let's go and find Syd and Janice, and head home." With that they scurried off.

"Boom!" cried out Gez, "Two-nil on the night to the loser brigade!" He gave Ruby a massive cuddle and a kiss.

Ruby was certainly pleased! What a night! "What goes around comes around."

Polly and Peter joined in for a massive 'Team Loser' hug. This night was off the scale! Ruby was so pleased she'd had the party! The best bit about tonight was deciding to invite The Bitches.

Chantelle and Siobhan headed back into the main party. They weren't buzzing any more. They'd got over the first round of abuse, but two lots of embarrassment in one night was simply too much to handle. Siobhan, who had got her mate back into the party spirit the first time, was reeling after what had just happened. Chantelle had totally lost the plot. "I can't fucking believe it! Let's get Janice and get the fuck out of here!"

"Where *is* Janice, Chantelle? Come to think of it, what happened to Syd?"

"I think they went to the toilet, but that was ages ago."

They decided to go and look for them. The party room was in full swing, in anticipation of the band coming on, and they were in no mood to party now. They pushed their way out of the room, and walked towards the toilets. No sign of them anywhere. Siobhan had gone down there earlier, and stumbled across the games room. Perhaps they were having a game of snooker or something? Syd liked a game of snooker. They tried the door. It was dark inside. Chantelle called out, "Janice? Syd? Are you in here?"

At the same time, Siobhan turned the light switch on. Siobhan's face screwed up as Janice sighed "Oh my god!"

Janice was bent over the snooker table, and Syd was behind her, giving her his all. Or rather he had been, but now he was motionless. Siobhan was a fairly big woman, with a bad temper when pushed, and she casually walked over to Syd and punched him squarely on the nose. He literally fell to the floor. She turned to Janice. "I can see who your sugar-daddy is now, you bitch." She punched Janice. Janice didn't flinch, but just took the punch.

Chantelle was with Siobhan. "You utter bastards! Come on Siobhan!"

They left the room. Chantelle was about to say something, but Siobhan got in first. "Don't say a fucking word Chantelle!"

Syd had a look of panic on his face. He couldn't believe it. Why did he do it? At the party! What was he thinking? He pulled up his trousers and rushed after Siobhan. He didn't say a word to Janice.

Janice was thinking 'Well, I guess that's the end of my gravy train.' If only Syd had stayed with her, or just said something! He was too worried about losing half his business, and all of his house. She bent down, pulled her knickers up smartly, and casually walked out.

Siobhan and Chantelle headed through the main room and through the kitchen. Syd came running after them. "Siobhan, I can explain."

She wasn't having any of it, and pushed people out of the way, closely followed by Chantelle. Everyone in the kitchen looked on as the drama unfolded. Ruby was perplexed. "What was *that* all about?"

Janice walked into the kitchen, with an expressionless face. She grabbed a bottle of vodka, necked about a quarter of it, put the bottle back down, and scanned the room, realising that everyone was looking at her. She addressed them all. "The moral of the story is, never have an affair with one of your best mates' husbands." She paused. "If you do, make sure you don't get caught shagging him at a party." She took another swig of the vodka. "Any smart arse wants to say anything will be wearing this bottle." She clocked Ruby looking at her, acknowledged her, then left. What she hadn't realised was that when she pulled her knickers back up, she'd got her skirt caught up in them. That was why most people were looking at her. A very nice arse shot!

Gez turned to Ruby. "Boom! This night is *full* of surprises!"

Ruby was incredulous. "So, Syd was her sugar-daddy! Oh my god! Didn't think he had it in him!"

"She had a good little money stream coming her way, but having to sleep with Syd... She obviously thought it was worth it, Ruby."

It was turning out to be a fantastic night for Ruby. All the years of abuse she'd endured at school were finally paling into insignificance. Just when she thought the night couldn't possibly get any better, the music stopped in the other room, and the sound of a band getting ready to play came drifting through. Ruby loved a good ska/punk band and Gez, unbeknownst to Ruby, had come up trumps. He smiled at Ruby. She looked so happy and complete. "Ruby, I did a bit of work for a guy in LA. I told him I didn't want paying for the job, but asked him if his band could play a few songs at your party. When I told him you had changed your name to the title of one of his songs, and told him your life story, he was over the moon."

Just then, the band's singer cried out "This one is for you, Ruby!" The song 'Ruby Soho' kicked in.

"Oh my god, Gez!"

They went running into the party room. Rancid, Ruby's favourite band, were playing. "Gez, this is the best day of my life! Apart from the day Polly came along!" She gave him a massive hug, then quickly got to the front, to dance. Wurzel, Lurch and Half A Man were going mental, dancing. The whole crowd was. Most of Ruby's mates used to be punks, and none of them could believe that Rancid were here playing.

Polly looked on at her mum and friends enjoying themselves. She liked a bit of punk herself, but she just wanted to capture the moment. Peter was surprised that these old English folk could dance like this, fifty-year olds acting like they were eighteen again.

The band eventually finished, and the DJ started up again. Nobody wanted to go home, and the party went on and on.

It finally faded out about 6 a.m. Most people thanked Ruby, and headed home. Others tidied up a bit, then crashed wherever they could. Ruby wasn't tired. She just kept tidying up for a couple of hours, while people slept around her. She was drinking plenty of water to clear her head, and plenty of coffee to keep her going.

You don't get many days in life when everything just clicks into place, and last night had been one of those. All her friends had come. At school they had struggled. They didn't fit in. Last night was their night. The bullies from school had finally been laid to rest. They were the ones who'd ended up with shallow lives. It's not *what* you have in life that counts, it's *who* you have in your life that's important. Without real friends, you are nothing.

Ruby decided to make some tea, coffee, and bacon sandwiches. It was time everyone got up. She took a tray into the TV room, where most of her close friends were sleeping. "Wakey wakey you lot!" It took a bit of time, but people began to stir. She then headed round all the rooms, getting people up. As you get older, you tend to get up earlier. Gone are the days of lying in bed all morning. Half the battle is that you need to get up for a wee, and once you are up you might as well stay up.

Lurch started playing with the remote for the television. He was looking to put the news or the sport on. The first thing that came up was the party room from last night. The remote handset controlled all the recordings from different rooms. "Ruby, what's this?" he asked.

"Oh, I had cameras put in all the rooms. I thought if it was a good party, I could edit it all together, and give you lot a copy. And before you ask, Lurch, there are no cameras in the bedrooms. I'm not that sick!"

Wurzel had awoken, looking mighty rough and feeling a bit cold. He still had no top or trousers on. Ruby nipped upstairs and brought him down some jogging pants and a jumper. "Here you go, Wurzel. I found your clothes and stuck them in the washing machine this morning. I think everyone at the party had been dancing on top of them."

Gez and Peter came in, wearing matching pyjamas that could only be described as looking like 'Rupert The Bear' costumes. Half A Man, who was half-awake, nursing a sore head, was the first to react, in his own inimitable style. "Jesus fucking Christ! I must have had too much to drink last night! I swear two Rupert The Bears just walked in. Are we having honey for breakfast?"

This got a bit of a laugh even from Peter. "You see, Gez, I told you this design would work! Any reaction is better than no reaction."

Polly now came into the room, looking very chuffed with herself. "Great party, Mum! Who's that in the corner?" Someone was asleep, wrapped up in bin liners. You couldn't see who it was. Polly gave him a little kick, but there was no reaction. She shrugged her shoulders, as if to say 'who knows?'

Lurch was still playing with the remote. Pictures from outside the front door, hallway, kitchen and then the games room. Oh my god! This got everyone's attention!

It was Half A Man, sitting at the end of the snooker table, with his back to the camera. He turned around and gave a cheeky grin and a thumbs-up to the camera. Everyone was a little confused as to what he was doing. Then you saw someone getting up in front of him. It was Siobhan, wiping her mouth.

"Way to go, Half A Man!" said Gez, admiringly.

There was a massive cheer from everyone, and Half A Man took a bow. "You ain't the only one she picked on at school, Ruby. Revenge!"

Lurch fast-forwarded the action. Next, it was Janice and Syd putting on a show. Everyone was howling with laughter, especially when Siobhan and Chantelle arrived. They all agreed that Janice could take a punch. Half lowered the tone. "Looks like she can take *most* things very well!"

That room had obviously seen a lot of action last night. Lurch fast-forwarded it some more. Next on the big screen was Polly and some bloke. Ruby wasn't too happy about this. "Lurch, turn that off now!" Everyone let out a boo. Polly was kissing the bloke, then stopped, took his hand, and left the room. Everyone booed again. Ruby looked relieved.

Polly was laughing. "Mum, I knew you had cameras in there." There was another collective boo. "So I shagged him upstairs!"

There was a big cheer from everyone, and even Ruby was laughing. Lurch fast-forwarded again, but nothing much else was happening. Ruby was thinking that she'd better wipe this clean, before it got onto social media.

Half was thinking something different. "Any chance of a copy of this, Ruby?"

They all wanted a copy, but she was having none of it. "I'll do you a copy of the band playing, and you lot all making fools of yourself, and that's it. No chance I'm letting this get out! You've got to be joking!"
Lurch has found something else. It was Chantelle, strutting up and down the snooker room. Someone entered. Lurch strained his eyes to see who it was. "Is that Johnny The Cab? Was Johnny here last night?"

A hand went up in the corner of the room. The person who'd been asleep, wrapped up in bin liners, was Johnny The Cab himself. On the screen, he put his hand in his pocket, and pulled out a plastic bag full of white powder. "That fell out of her bag in my cab earlier," he shouted out. Back on the screen, he held the bag up above head height, waving it about. She tried to grab it, but he wouldn't let her have it. A discussion took place, she nodded, and he handed over the bag. She was then out of shot, probably snorting a line. She came back into shot, pulled up her dress, pulled down her knickers, and gave them to him. Johnny seemed happy with that, and was about to leave, when she grabbed him and kissed him. He looked like he wasn't interested, but she persisted, and in the end, he succumbed.

It was a bit weird. Everyone was confused. "I fancied that woman from when I was about fifteen", he explained. "She was in all the lingerie sections of the catalogue. I just wanted her knickers. I don't know why. I've shagged her in my dreams many a time, and I just didn't want to spoil the illusion. In fairness, it wasn't bad." He pulled out the knickers and waved them around, to rapturous applause.

Ruby turned to Gez. "Can I be fifty every week?"

THE END

About Kevee Lynch

Kevee has worked within the building and Landscaping trade all of his working career.

He has a zest for life and has performed with many bands over the years.

He currently fronts the Ska-Punk band SKo-mAds.

He cycled across America with friends and wrote a book entitled Route 66 Cycle Challenge, Kevee's Story, back in 2013.

A keen radio listener, he ended up presenting the very successful "Wake Up With Kevee" on Saturday mornings for his local radio station.

Coming shortly: The Underdog stories volume 2

Lightning Source UK Ltd.
Milton Keynes UK
UKOW05f0616030217

293507UK00001B/180/P